ACKNOWLEDGMENTS

Frédérique Delacoste and Felice Newman chose me to helm this incredible series for yet another installment, and for this I am honored, grateful, and ridiculously happy—thank you; our relationship means more than I can express here. My deepest feelings are reserved for my family—Survival Research Laboratories and Mark Pauline. My love always belongs to my close friends: Courtney, Thomas, Annalisa, Xeni, Simone, Chriso and everyone else who touches my heart. Also—for Bre.

CONTENTS

INTRODUCTION:
LUST, CONQUER, SEE

I often think of editing an erotic anthology like curating a gallery exhibition. To put together a powerful show, you have to examine dozens (or in this case, hundreds) of selections and cull the strongest pieces. And each piece needs to be considered in the context of the whole; a good curator will pick a handful of talented big names and hang them with a roster of startling new discoveries.

With erotica, the art of selection is even more personal. In choosing the pieces for *Best Women's Erotica 2007*, I tried to imagine how each story might reach into the core of a reader's sexuality, find the trigger, and pull it.

I approached each piece as I might approach a fantastic painting or a jaw-dropping drawing or a visceral photograph, allowing it to overtake my senses, my imagination—and yes, my pussy. This collection did something to me while I was putting it together. The stories here provoked me. They took me over. Bits of them found me in the middle of the night when I couldn't sleep; they visited me during the day on my way to the local café; they left me feeling that I wanted more. Was I hungry? Was I thirsty? Was I obsessed with the little details about slick fingers inside panties, a rough fuck by a tattooed boy who loves to spank while he probes, or women paying for outrageous sexual fetishes that most don't even dare to speak of? I wasn't sure. But I wanted more.

In "To Serge with Love," by Reen Guierre, a young woman's relationship with a British author goes from cybersex to phone sex to an outrageous first-time meeting in person, complete with an unusual (and inspiring) sex toy trick that leaves him literally breathless. In "Inked," Jordana Winters follows a fascination many of us have for tattooed boys to an incendiary conclusion. "Chill," by Kathleen Bradean, is one of the edgiest, most outrageous fetish sex stories I've had the pleasure of reading over and over. It arouses you as much as it holds your attention rapt in disbelief that such a taboo could be so—hot.

"This Flesh Has Changed Meaning," by Jennifer Cross, takes the rushed yet tender fuck between two new mothers to dizzy heights; Jean Casse's "Hands" gives us a most delectable butch who seduces a straight girl only to find that her lust for hands leads her farther than she'd ever thought she'd go—onto her new lover's boyfriend's fist. In "Cowboy," Rita Rollins shows what happens when a lap dancer indulges her fantasies with a client in a most unconventional way, making boundaries into sex toys for the rest of us. "Rhythm Like a

Heartbeat," by Sophie Mouette, makes dancing into a new and delicious sex act when a woman decides her curvy hips should move in time with her heart—and her pussy—with thigh-clenching results.

Jane Black's "Pivot" is one of this show's tricks of the light: As you begin it you might think it's just another hot power exchange fantasy, but when the angle shifts for our female protagonist, so does the sexual control. "Fluid Humiliation," by Kayla Kuffs, may just be the Mapplethorpe in our collection, as a woman agrees to an ever-surprising level of enema humiliation play—and yes, it's just as surprising (even to her) as it is a turn-on. "Becky," by Kay Jaybee, is our most playful selection and one of the joys of the collection, even if that joy arrives with the tongue-in-cheek stripes of a cane properly applied in the most unusual office in the history of cubicle farms. Don't let Irma Wimple's "Electric Razor" make you think that women are all about appliances and power tools—except when we are, in the most devious ways.

In "Just Words," Donna George Storey appeals to the snarkiest in all of us when a woman decides to play along halfheartedly with her lover's phone sex games, until the words (as they are wont to do) take over her hands, her control, and her orgasms. Thea Hutchinson's "Galatea Broached" combines lush imagery, male observation, and female sexual awakening in a stunning vista of pure voyeuristic adventure. In "Call Me," by Kristina Wright, a wrong number turns into the right amount of filthiness for a repeat encounter. Scarlett French's "Play Spaces" is a snapshot of a newcomer's night in a sex club, with each new room as thrilling and arousing for her as the last.

"Voice of an Angel," by Teresa Noelle Roberts, is the

baroque centerpiece of this erotic exhibition, in which a costume designer discovers that an opera singer's voice penetrates more than her ears—culminating in a riveting oral scenario. One woman's overwhelming urge to conquer male skin with her voracious vulva makes "Puffy Lips," by Susie Hara, a story you'll want to revisit. Alison Tyler's "Worth It" is a powerful portrait of a woman on the verge of marriage who is derailed by her desire for taboo anal sex. And if you've ever been consumed with the desire to fuck so hard that it burns through your skin and makes you into something not quite human, then you'll be unable to walk away from Rachel Kramer Bussel's "Animals" unchanged.

There is quite a show for you here, and I promise it will leave you wanting more.

Violet Blue
August 2006

TO SERGE WITH LOVE

Reen Guierre

"I can't wait to be with you, to smell behind your ears and lick your ass. I want to see you more excited than you have ever been in your life." She breathed heavily into the phone, and she could just make out the muffled slapping noise as he masturbated furiously to her filthy discourse from the other side of the ocean. He was a man of the world, and yet in so many ways, he was naive. He hadn't ever had anything more than a finger in his ass, though she could tell by the way he whimpered when she spoke of fucking him that he wanted it badly.

"Serge, I want you to think about how good you're going to feel when we're all alone. You're going to make me come, over and over, and when I finally allow you to come, it will be the best imaginable. I'll see you next week, Sphinx." She pressed the Off button and left him to come on his own.

She called him Sphinx because that was his screen name. He was a photographer who specialized in the ruins and artifacts of ancient cultures. He worked for magazines and popular scientific journals most of his career, but now had written a book of his own. Well, actually, it was more of a large-format picture book of his photographs. He sent her pdfs of a sampling of pages and they were fascinating. There was a complete world full of sexual artifacts found in nearly every culture that had ever lived and walked on the earth. But, because of our society's tendency to suppress such things, the average person never got to see them. The vulvae carved in stone, the mosaics of men taking other men, and the frescoes intended to inform patrons of the various services offered by prostitutes, and their cost, were all unknown to the general public. Not to exclude all the wonderful phallic objects, in all sizes from miniature to obelisk, crafted in a myriad of different colors from a multitude of different materials. These were the things that never made it into the pages of *National Geographic*. These were the things that most Americans didn't know existed.

Elle had been having phone sex with him for about six months. Before that it was cybersex. All told, their relationship had been active for over a year. Elle found him interesting, to be sure, and he was so responsive when she pushed him around a bit, so to speak. Serge was scheduled to do a book signing at a bookstore in London and invited her over for it. She felt fairly confident that he wouldn't stand her, and the bookstore, up, so she accepted. Besides, she wasn't exactly the needy type who couldn't have a good time on her own if things didn't work out with him.

That night, and every night after, she thought about plea-suring Serge until he went mad, until he just couldn't take her stimulations anymore. She dreamed of meeting him in a room filled with sheer curtains and scented with sandalwood. There she turned him over onto a special table designed for whip-ping. In the dream, there didn't seem to be anything to whip him with, so she knelt down and spread his legs open wider and pushed her face forward so she could lick his balls from behind. His balls began those slow, involuntary contractions she was always fascinated to observe.

Four days later, she was enduring the eight-hour flight from Minneapolis to London with the help of two tiny bottles of Skyy, dispensed by the flight attendant every time she woke up. The redeye, provided one could sleep, landed at Gatwick at eight in the morning, so chances of suffering from jet lag were minimized. She deliberately chose Gatwick over Heathrow because she'd never had her luggage searched there. She knew that if one of the unfailingly handsome young men from security came across the little purple vibrating butt plug she had purchased for Serge, she would have to stand there and wait while the man turned it on, looked inside it, and rifled through her clothes looking for the rest of her cache. She made a mental picture of a tall young lad holding the crop in one hand and the butt plug in the other. It wasn't so much that she was embarrassed, but there were enough queues to wait in without looking for more.

Serge had offered her his flat to stay in, but she'd refused and made reservations at a boutique hotel in Kensington. It was an ideal location. She could walk through the park almost end-lessly in several directions, go to a concert at the Albert Hall, spend an afternoon perusing special exhibits at the V&A, or catch the South Kensington tube to anywhere else—perhaps Soho, with its plenitude of women-friendly adult shops. She purchased a travel card to use the four days she would be in London, beginning with the train ride from Gatwick to Victoria, then a short tube ride to South Kensington.

Elle was relieved to make it past the random luggage check and was wheeling her case down the ramp, home free, when she caught sight of her name on a card. It was Serge. He had come to pick her up at the airport even though she specifically told him she preferred to get to her hotel on her own.

She knew they would recognize each other because they'd sent many pictures, via e-mail, over the past year. What she hadn't expected was to feel a surge of excitement when his eyes found hers. He lowered the card to reveal his attractive face. He had bratty lips and coloring and a nose that betrayed a Roman ancestor. She walked directly to him, and when she stood before him, he reached up to kiss her on the cheek. Instead of letting him, she made a quarter turn to avoid him. She offered the handle of her case for him to take and said, in a commanding voice, "Walk behind me."

She didn't look back, but she knew he was right behind her. Walking down corridor after corridor, she could hear the squeak of the little wheels of her suitcase. Suddenly, she spun around, placed her hands on his chest, and pushed him into an alcove between the windows of the wide hallway. She used her weight to press him into the shadowed space while a continuous stream of people flowed behind them. She said, "Many women love surprises. I don't. Do you understand?"

He nodded and looked into her face. His eyes revealed a little fear and a lot of love. She began pulling his shirt out from under his belt so her hands could feel his bare chest.

She moved her hands over his tiny nipples and pinched them between her knuckles, pulling until she lost her grip and they snapped back. He was obviously excited, but frightened at the same time. He feared being caught in an awkward situation, but he was desperate for her touch. She was the most exciting thing that had ever happened to him. From the first time she typed an instant message to him, he was hooked. Since then, an hour hadn't gone by without his fantasizing about sex with her. He harbored ideas of a permanent relationship and wanted to please her so she would stay.

His eyes left hers so he could see if they were attracting any attention from passersby. She shoved him harder into the corner, and he knew that he must not do that again. His eyes gazed into hers without wavering this time. She kissed his generous lips before releasing him, and he felt so grateful for the contact.

He hoisted the case into the trunk of the car and drove her to her hotel. He waited while she checked in, not at all sure that she would be inviting him up. When she'd finished with the paperwork he heard her tell the woman behind the counter that she would not be needing help with her suitcase. He brightened at that. She did, apparently, want him to carry her case to her room. They both entered the small, brightly lit room with the steeple of the church next door visible through the lace curtains.

Serge put down her case and they stood looking at each other for a second. Elle said, "Take your pants down."

He followed her direction. Once again he was excited and nervous at the same time. He opened the button and unzipped, then pulled his trousers and shorts down around his knees.

She couldn't see his cock behind his shirttails. She walked

around to survey his rear and, when she saw it, had to suppress a lustful gasp. He had the sexiest ass she had ever seen. His cheeks were the size and shape of powder puffs she'd gotten as gifts when she was young. Those powder puffs were so precious and fancy, kept under their tinted plastic domes meant to look like cut glass. His skin was as white and smooth as the powder. She knelt down behind him and he groaned in anticipation. She told him to spread his cheeks open with his fingers so she could inspect his little asshole in the light of the morning sun. The smell of tangerines met her nostrils. He had prepared himself for her.

His entire crack was a smoky charcoal color, completely hidden when his snow-white cheeks were closed. His asymmetrical, little puckered opening was just what she had envisioned, and hoped for. She hungrily lunged for his crevice and tongued, licked, and ate to her delight. He squirmed and made little "uh" noises throughout the mastication of his most private of parts. He could barely stay standing by the time she was finished with him, for his legs had turned to rubber.

She told him to take his clothes off completely and get down on his hands and knees. She opened her suitcase on the bed and pulled out the purple butt plug and some lubricant. He saw what she was doing and his mouth dropped open slightly, but he didn't move. She began by circling the plug over his anus. She turned on the vibrator to loosen up the virgin muscles of his asshole. His eyes were closed as he savored every sensation and tried to relax himself for her. She pushed the plug, stretching his sphincter, as the first bulb entered his waiting body. He responded with a long "ahh" sound, but didn't move forward at all. She licked the taut skin, expanded tightly around the toy, and told him he was almost there. She added more lube and pushed the second bulb into his gorgeous ass. His eyes stayed shut but his head craned back in a prayer to the god of pleasure. Without warning, she quickly pushed the last bulb into his ass and, to her delight, he backed into it. The device would rest in place with the flange on the outside, provided he didn't relax too much, so she told him he must work to keep it in place.

She pulled a chair up in front of him and sat in it. She raised up her skirt and his eyes fixated on her crotch. She slid her thong down around her knees and removed it, one foot at a time. She scooted forward in the chair and drew up her skirt to reveal her neatly trimmed cunt. The hair was half an inch long and completely tamed, following the contours of her pubic bone and lips. He lost his concentration and the plug slipped out a little. She went to her case again and pulled out a very thin, black vinyl cord. She tied the middle of it around the base of the toy and used the two long ends as reins. Elle sat back in the chair in front of his face and tugged on the reins, pulling the toy back into his rectum. He grunted a little and licked his lips. She positioned herself so he could perform with his tongue on the rose-colored ribbon inside her well-groomed outer lips. She told him how she wanted it, just the lightest touch at first, and then, when she was gyrating her hips, a bit stronger and faster.

He was never more excited in his life—be damned what they say about men when they're nineteen. Her cunt was musky smelling after sitting on the long flight, and it fueled his desire to please her as she was giving so much pleasure to him. He felt the butt plug still vibrating inside him, and that, plus the reins, made him feel he was participating in something very naughty and forbidden. He pursed his lips and sucked her whole labia into his mouth and swiped over the thin, soft skin with his tongue. This set off a powerful orgasm for her that surely must have been heard in the pub across the street.

She could see he was proud of his accomplishment and decided to fuck him right away. She had him stand while she held the plug in his ass. She gently fucked it in and out of him a little, and he seemed to enjoy it. Elle sat him down in the chair, which pushed the purple toy up as far as it would go, and again he groaned. She opened his shirt for the first time, exposing his beautiful cock. She straddled him, reached down to guide it in, and let her weight fall onto his lap. She raised and lowered herself, rubbing her cunt on his groin.

His eyes nearly rolled up into his head. He was being fucked in two places at once and he couldn't believe how good it felt. His ass was being violated with nonstop pulsing and his cock was being fucked by the woman he had fantasized about for a over a year. He made an attempt at thrusting and found he could tilt his pelvis forward and back slightly, giving himself a fucking sensation in his ass. It was glorious, and he matched her rhythm. His eyes met hers as he paid close attention to the timing of her orgasm. He knew that if he came and went soft before her cum serenade, she would not be pleased.

She was bucking more wildly over his groin, and she suspected he was ready to come as well. The thought of him with the toy inside, fucking her while he was being penetrated, pushed her over the edge and she came again with renewed force, squeezing every last sensation out of her orgasm. She looked down at him and he begged her with his eyes to come. She softened in her affection for him and began again to ride his very nice cock. He pushed up into her until he experienced the most satisfying release of mind, body, and fluid that he had ever felt.

Elle told him not to call, and he didn't. She didn't do any of the things she thought she might while in the city. Instead, she took a few tube rides and then switched to the Docklands Light Railway. She got off at Greenwich Cutty Sark and wandered around the dock for a while. This was one of the few places where there was a bit of shore and not just a steep wall that disappeared into the river. She headed for the park and climbed to the top of the hill, turning when she reached it, to take in the view. She was lucky—visibility was pretty good. The solid old observatory stood on the side of the cleared area. She continued her walk back to the deer park and couldn't resist bending down to pet a little dog that seemed to veer off toward her at exactly the same moment. The man on the other end of the lead giggled at his pet's synchronicity with a stranger. As quickly as she bent down, she stood and started walking again, never even seeing the man. She wandered around the gardens for a while and began to notice it was getting dark. She glanced at her watch, but it was still ten to two. The second hand was not moving. How odd, she thought, that her watch should stop where time begins.

The next evening was Serge's big book signing. She was completely unprepared for how big it actually turned out to be. When she arrived, there was a long line of people waiting for Serge's signature. Anything to do with sex was usually a big hit in London, whereas the Museum of Sex in New York City had to struggle by without even an answering machine.

Elle ducked out of the bookshop and found a quiet restaurant nearby. She sat next to the window in an overstuffed chair and sipped her drink, knowing what was coming, but not knowing exactly how she would respond. There was nothing tying her to the States. She was free to go where she liked. After being with Serge, she was more attracted to him than ever. She felt they had many adventures ahead of them, but she wasn't yet interested in a commitment.

After two drinks and watching several people walk by with Serge's book in their hands, she decided to go back to the store and queue up. She had timed it just right. There were only a few people ahead of her. He noticed Elle just as he was personalizing an elderly woman's copy in front of her. The lady scooped up the book and held it to her chest with both hands. She turned around and said to Elle, "I posed for one of these."

Elle smiled back and thought, Wow, ancient.

Serge took her book, and his eyes were beaming. He opened it to the dedication page and signed, *For Elle—friend, lover and partner.*

She spun the book around and said, "That's pretty intense. Did you write that on everyone's book?"

"Yes," he said. She noticed then that it was exactly how the printed dedication read.

"I know you don't like surprises, but I was thinking maybe you'd like to stay here with me. I'll marry you if it'll keep you in the country."

"I'd rather enter as a highly skilled immigrant, if you don't mind," she said.

"Wonderful," he said, smiling. Then a puzzled look came over his face. "What is it you do, anyway?"

"I thought you knew," she said. "I'm an exotic animal trainer."

INKED

Jordana Winters

"Sweet Jesus."

She set the remote down on the coffee table. She'd been aimlessly flipping through the channels. She'd stopped on TLC—some documentary about people heavily into tattoos, piercing, and body modification.

She squeezed her thighs together at the sight of a nicely built, fully tattooed bald guy on the TV.

"Fuck. I'd let him bend me over any day of the week," Carly muttered to herself.

Carly had fucked tattoo boys before, although in her estimation not nearly enough. On her list of boys to fuck, a guy with full sleeves and nearly covered with ink was up there as a priority. Make no mistake—at some point in her life she was going to find him.

Carly traced her fingertips over her stomach, outlining her own artwork. A black dragon decorated her belly: Celtic artwork wrapped around her hips and ended at her lower back. A pinup girl decorated each shoulder, with another Celtic piece adorning the area between her shoulder blades. It wasn't going to stop there. She had the rest of her body mapped out for more ornamentation.

Her fetish for tattooed boys started years ago and showed no signs of stopping. Unfortunately, they wore the bad-boy stereotype too well. If she could find herself one who didn't have aspirations of being a rock star and little else, who wasn't always "in between jobs," and who had more than two cents to rub together, she figured she'd be doing okay. In the meantime, she figured she could at least fuck them when the opportunity presented itself.

Carly grabbed the phone and dialed her lover's number. Their relationship had been on-again, off-again since they'd started dating. They were together but they weren't, but whatever—it suited her. She neither wanted nor needed his love. She was more than capable of keeping things simple.

Bailey picked up on the third ring. He was at work and due to get off within the half hour.

"Hey," she purred.

"Hey. What's up?"

"What are you doing after work?" she asked.

"Nothing planned."

"You want to come over?"

"Sure. I'll be there in a bit. I gotta jet. I'm doing the books," he explained.

"Okay. See ya in a bit," she said, and hung up.

She supposed their relationship wasn't all about sex. They

did enjoy each other's company. Together they watched movies, went to concerts, and went out drinking. Nine times out of ten, they'd end up in the sack, probably because she was sexually attracted to him to the point of ridiculousness. There was a level of emotional detachment on both their sides, but she'd long ago decided that as long as she was getting something out of the relationship, it suited her.

An hour later he was at her place, sitting on her couch, and recounting stories about his day.

"I'm beat," he said, and reached for the TV remote.

"Not too tired, I hope," she purred, sliding her foot to his crotch, which she rubbed through his jeans.

"You know I'm never too tired for that."

For the first time in her life she'd met a man whose sexual appetite matched her own. She'd never known a man who could get a hard-on as fast as he could, and be ready to fuck at the drop of a hat.

She moved to sit on top of him, her legs straddling him. Her fingers traced the lines of his sideburns down his neck to the tattoo that peeked out from under his shirt.

"You're horny," he stated.

"Is it that obvious?"

"It is. I can see it in your eyes. Why so horny?"

"Not sure," she lied, thinking of the tattooed boys on the TV earlier.

She grabbed hold of the thick necklace of chain he had around his neck and pulled him to her. She kissed him forcefully, pushing him into the couch as she ran her fingers through the back of his hair, something that was always guaranteed to emit a groan of pleasure from him.

His hands moved to her breasts, which he squeezed roughly

through her thin shirt. They sank sideways on the couch until he was lying on top of her. She wrapped her legs around his waist and ground her sex against his crotch.

They peeled each other's clothes off, slowly at first, then growing more frenzied. He teased her sex through her panties, rubbing at her gently, knowing just the right amount of pressure to make her squirm. He slid her panties slowly down her thighs. Then he slid his fingers into her wetness. He rubbed her clit with his thumb and finger-fucked her until she was ready to come. Then he stopped, as he often did, just to tease.

She rolled on top of him and rained kisses down his chest, stopping to bite and pinch his nipples. She bit at the skin of his belly, something she'd learned long ago that he enjoyed. She lapped at his balls and cockhead but didn't take him in her mouth.

He grabbed her by the back of her hair and pulled her head roughly to the side.

"Stop," he grunted and flipped her over so she was lying on her side.

A hand wrapped tightly around her throat as his fingers slid into her sex and opened her for his cock to follow. She meowed out a "fuck" as his grip tightened harder still around her throat and his cock entered her fully in one slow thrust.

She turned her head, laying her cheek against the soft material of the couch, and glanced up at him. She thought he was the sexiest motherfucker alive when he was fucking her. Both his arms were partially covered in tattoos, and some of his chest and neck as well. The sight of his tats and his pierced nipple, septum, and ears was hot enough without the sex.

She reached around behind him and grabbed hold of his

ass cheek, pulling him closer to her, coaxing him to fuck her harder.

His grip tightened around her throat until she was having a hard time catching her breath. His thrusts grew harder, almost hurting her, but he was unrelenting, knowing he wasn't quite at the point where she considered it too rough.

He released her throat and gripped the skin of her ass, while his other hand lubed the rim of her asshole with her wetness. Then, a thumb or finger, she neither knew nor cared, slipped into her ass, invading her pleasantly with its thickness.

"You like that?" he growled from behind her, pinching the skin of her ass harder.

To be nothing other than difficult, she didn't answer.

"Do you like that?" he asked again, forcefully.

His hand snaked around to her sex as he slowed his thrusting to a deliberate tease. His fingers easily traced and teased over her clit, his fingers wet from her juices. Pulses of heat radiated through her sex.

"You fuckin' like it."

Her ass cheeks shook against his skin. His fingertip stroked her clit harder. With her help, he'd been a quick study in learning how to get her to come.

She cried out as her sex pulsed in intense radiating waves.

His finger stopped its invasion of her ass and instead gently caressed her asshole. Then he was thrusting into her again, hard and fast. He was going to come.

His fingers bit into the skin of her shoulder as he shuddered above her. He buried his cock in her, and she felt his balls pulse as he came.

"Fuck," he muttered through what sounded like clenched teeth.

She loved when he came. His coming was easily predictable and very vocal. She could never get bored of it. He didn't hold anything back. It was hot to feel and hear him come so hard.

"Ugggghh," he groaned as he fell off her, moving her away from the couch.

His cum leaked out from between her thighs. Not wanting to stain the couch, she stood up and walked to her bedroom, with him at her heels. Together, they collapsed on the bed and lay on their backs. He reached out and grabbed for her hand, which took his and held it tightly. She smiled at his small act of sweetness.

"You hungry?" she asked him, after several quiet minutes. She released his hand and stood up.

"You've got to stop feeding me. You spoil me."

"I know I do."

And she did, but she didn't really mind it.

"Hang on. Come here," he said, holding up his hand.

She grabbed it and fell on top of him. He kissed her while reaching around and grabbing a handful of her ass.

"You still have any of those chicken balls?"

"I do. They'll be done in twenty," she said, kissed him again, and stood up.

She stopped at the door and turned to look at him. Fuck. Yes. Those goddamn tattoos.

"Carly. That was hot, but—it always is," he said and smiled at her.

"I know."

CHILL

Kathleen Bradean

I could have gone home, but they had my six hundred dollars.

Even though I could have told them that I changed my mind, I could imagine the lifted eyebrow, and the apologetic, "Very well, Madame, perhaps we can accommodate you another time," but it was the last time I would visit the spa to indulge my fetish. There was no sense in canceling what had already begun, though. I would use it up. Then there would be no more. I wouldn't give myself any more.

Outside the room, three stories down, I heard cars drive through slush. I pushed aside the heavy drapes to look at the busy street below. Windshields on the cars were fogged as heaters ran full blast. People fled home, to bars, to fireplaces and central heat, to life, to warmth.

The discreet townhouse masquerading as a spa for wealthy women was old. Cold air seeped past the windowpanes. I pressed my hands to the flawed glass that made the brake lights look like smeared lipstick.

If I listened, I could hear the elevated trains one block away. And if I peered just right through the narrow slit between the buildings across the street, I could see the darkness of Lake Michigan, inviting me under.

In the room assigned to me, the bed frame was wrought iron. A crimson coverlet hinted at lurid delights, but it wasn't my fantasy to be fucked in velvet splendor. The Victorian trappings seemed pathetic, even cheap, although the wallpaper was probably authentic and the antique chairs were worth more than my car.

I'd searched the drawers of the Chippendale dresser earlier. Masks, handcuffs, paddles—the props of theatrical fantasies. I was disappointed that given a chance to explore the unthinkable at the spa, most women opted instead for a hack rehash. Or maybe I was jealous of how harmless it all seemed. How comfortable. After a third martini, confessing to a spanking and a ride on one of the legendary cocks of the spa was probably de rigueur for the ladies who lunched.

"Antonio? Dear, you absolutely must try him. His dick curves a little, but it hits exactly the right spot when you're bent over the bed, taking it from behind. Trust me."

"If you pay extra, George won't bathe for three days. Get your nose up against those balls and take a whiff. I swear you can smell his boyfriend's ass."

I'll teach myself to crave such tame moments. I'll learn to clutch raw silk between my fingers and marvel at the texture. I'll develop a taste for opulence.

I used silver tongs to pick five ice cubes from the bucket. They clinked into the highball glass, each one making the crystal sing a slightly different note.

It was a matter of degree, really. Kink was candy coating that made sex tastier. Fetish was bittersweet, dark chocolate, straight up, the kind that made your teeth shrink against the intensity of undiluted flavor.

Fetish was sex deconstructed. Removed from my body to my mind. The rites of worship worshipped. The fetish was for the details. Someone once said that God was in the details, but others said that it was the devil. A devil I knew intimately.

I went into the bathroom and turned on the cold tap. The edge of the claw-foot tub made an uncomfortable seat. I set the highball glass in the soap dish and dropped the thick terry robe to the white tiled floor.

While the bath filled, I pulled back my hair in a severe ponytail high on my head, revealing every line on my face to the unflattering light at the makeup table in the boudoir.

First, I did my nails, hands, and feet. Light purple traced a thin line near my cuticles. Pale blue made a half-moon at the base of each nail. Blue-tinged varnish sealed it. For the last time, every single thing had to be just perfect. That way, if I felt myself sliding back, wanting it, I'd be able to remind myself that for once everything was right and exactly the way it should have been, and I could never hope to duplicate such perfection again.

No one I knew would recognize the brand of makeup in my bag. I used a thick, oily base, a shade paler than my natural coloring, and spread it thickly so that it left an obvious line under my chin and by my temples. Every wrinkle around my mouth and eyes showed like sidewalk crack. Blue lipstick made my mouth looked bruised. I drew another set of lips, slightly smaller, in dark pink on top of that, so that the edges of blue showed. Cherry rouge started as circles on my cheeks and then faded in a slight upstroke.

The first step into the tub was always hardest, like swimming in a mountain lake at camp. My foot ached and I wanted to pull it out, but I stepped in with the other foot, gritted my teeth, and sank into the deep, frigid water.

My skin pulled tight on my arms. Gooseflesh made every hair stand on end. I bent my knees. Gasping, I got my shoulders under the surface. My poor nipples hardened and ached. Fighting the shock, my heart pumped hot blood under my skin. My teeth chattered, uncontrollable. I reached for my highball glass.

My cunt tightened, refusing to take the ice cubes, but I pushed four in anyway. I felt my heat flee to my core. My toes and fingers throbbed and then burned.

"I hate this." My voice echoed off the bathroom tiles. I hate this, and I'm never going to do it again. If I'm tempted, this will be the part I'll make myself remember. The part I hate.

Cold. I was so fucking cold. My pussy longed to push out the cubes tucked into it, but every time one floated to the surface of the water, I pushed it back in, deep, until my knuckles pressed against my clit.

The shuddering came next. It exhausted me as no workout with my personal trainer ever had. I clamped down, refusing to let my muscles create more heat. The ice that worked out of me melted to such small slivers that I couldn't find them in the water. My fingertips were leaden as they clumsily tested my internal temperature. There was heat, but only deep inside. My clit was tight. It hurt to touch.

I should leave now. I should drain this freezing water away and pour scalding water over my skin until the burn hurts as much as the cold, until my skin is mottled pink. I should pick up the phone and tell them I've changed my mind, that I want a different fantasy this time, something red and violent, a fuck that will leave my pussy raw. Something normal.

I tipped back my head and let it rest on the folded towel on the back of the tub. The walls of the bathroom had a bluish cast, like icebergs. White seemed a final color, but like black, it had shades, tones, subtleties. When I stared at it long enough, flecks of green, red, and blue danced in the center of my vision.

A drop fell from the silver faucet into the bath, a hollow, metallic sound followed by a rich plop. Ripples pushed across the surface of the water. The water lapped at the underside of my chin.

Ah, well. What was done, was done. I was there. It was in motion. I picked up the highball glass and let the last cube clink from side to side, sweeping out time. Then I plucked it out and shoved it inside me as I exhaled.

I rose from the water, letting it drip, before carefully blotting it away with the thick towels. It took several conversations to convince the house staff that I didn't want heated towels waiting.

When I was dry, I dropped the towels on the floor and opened the other door. Air conditioning rushed against my skin. My nipples puckered to hard, erect rouge nubs. Perfect.

Unlike the bedroom, the other room was stark. Three of the walls were painted glossy white. Large stainless-steel drawers seemed to line the back wall from floor to ceiling, but I knew from exploration that they didn't open. Fantasy only went so far.

In the center of the room was one stainless-steel table. A single, thin white sheet sat folded at the foot. On top of it was a tag. I knew that underneath the table, there were stirrups. The one drawer on the side of the table held enema nozzles. With few alterations, any medical scene could be played out. I hated to think of anyone else using my sterile room, but I doubted the spa kept it just for me.

The floor tiles were cold against the bottom of my feet. The table was a chilled slab and my fingerprints made brief appearances on the brushed surface before disappearing like ghosts. I climbed awkwardly onto it.

I took the tag and placed the loop over my big toe before lying down with my legs spread wide so that Devon's legs wouldn't touch mine when he knelt between my thighs. The overhead mirror was unkind, so I only looked in glances at my pale skin, my carefully positioned body, my death mask. Then I unfurled the crisp sheet and pulled it over my body until it covered my face.

I could see the four bulbs of the overhead light fixture through the sheet. I closed my eyes tight and hoped he'd hurry. We didn't have much time. Every detail was perfection. It would never be this good again. Never.

At the soft click of the door, I opened my eyes again. Every breath was smooth, shallow, measured. I willed myself to relax, to give up control.

Devon was well trained. Although I stared at the ceiling, I knew that he gave my face only a glance as he folded the sheet down to the swell of my breasts. The bare warmth of the sheet escaped as he lifted the sheet from my feet and folded it above my waist, exposing the spider's veins on my calves, the cottage cheese texture of my outer thighs, the fluff of pubic hair carefully confined by waxing to a strip on my outer lips. Only then did he pull on examination gloves.

He put his gloved hand on the table.

Would he jump if I moved?

Devon climbed on the table. I stared past the overhead mirror, but I saw he was dressed in white scrubs. He lowered the waistband and freed his cock. Carefully balancing so that no part of his body touched mine, he pumped generous lube into the palm of his gloved hand.

My nipples ached in the cold air and my toes throbbed. So cold. I wanted to shiver. My skin pulled tight against my bones.

So many shades of white, like textures, all of them different.

I heard the wet slide of his fist over his cock.

Shame rose in a warm glow in my cheeks. It wouldn't show through the thick base, but it was there. Heat.

It wasn't healthy, this thing, this need. I'd go for months without it, and then I'd be on the phone with a client, or at dinner with friends, and I'd yearn for the cold. Thinking about it would make my breasts ache. I'd cross and uncross my legs, and fidget in my chair. Sometimes, I'd take an ice cube from my drink, put in into my mouth, and excuse myself to the ladies room, where I'd rub the cube against my clit until I came. Then I'd smooth down my clothes and take my seat, and no one would ever guess. But it was never a really good orgasm. It was a shadow, a knockoff, a little something to see me through.

When I first came to the spa, the entire staff was displayed for me. One by one, the nude men entered the room and showed me their bodies, their hard-ons, their secret tattoos. My purse sat in my lap and my hand rested on top of it until the last man joined the lineup, discreetly waiting for approval. In their own way, each one was perfection. Cute, handsome, pretty, pouty, tough, nasty, clean-cut, muscled, slim, slight, towering, hairy, smooth—they were all ideal.

"Which ones take direction well?"

"All of our—"

With a simple movement of my hand, I cut off the flow of words. "I don't want a sexual submissive, or a man who pretends to be one. I want someone who can correctly follow very detailed instructions. Intelligence is a plus." I turned my head. "And he must consistently shoot a big load."

Devon was not the best-endowed member on staff, his looks didn't excite me, and he was not the one I would have picked for recreational fucking, but he met my requirements.

He was quiet while he jerked off. A few gasps, the slap of his hand, and the squishy sound of the lube was all I heard. I should have told him that it was okay to make noise. Or maybe all men were that silent while stroking themselves to climax.

Don't blink.

A trickle of water from the melting ice cube streamed out of my pussy and pooled under my butt cheek.

My eyeballs were dry. Halos from the light fixture to the side of the overhead mirror seemed permanently seared into my retinas.

The air conditioner kicked on again, fighting the heat given off by the friction of Devon's hand on his cock. Chill air rasped against my skin. I fought the need to shudder.

Yes, remember this. Remember how much you hate what it takes to get the details right. Next time you're tempted to pick up the phone and make an appointment, remember that it hurts to have ice cubes in your cunt. Think of the pain in your feet and hands. Think about never being warm again.

In the overhead mirror, if I allowed myself to focus, I could see his black curls bobbing and the dip of his shoulder with every stroke. I'd see the purplish head of his dick strangled by his gloved hand, the slide of the foreskin until he was so hard that it wouldn't pass his glans. He'd bowed his head to the task and I was tempted to sneak a glance at his face, to see the concentration, to love him for the utter selfishness, but I refused to look. Everything had to be just right this last time.

He groaned. The table shook as he worked his cock. He knew not to waste time. With his free hand, Devon spread my labial lips. Warmth bled through the gloves to my skin.

Devon whispered something, maybe a prayer, and grunted. He hissed through clenched teeth.

Hot, thick cum splattered against my clit. I bit my tongue to hold back my moan. He came buckets, my Devon did, covering my cunt like boiling water splashed on snow. Another shot, so warm, so full of life, pulsed onto my chilled skin. It slid from the hard nub of my clit down toward my pussy. My clit tingled under it, loving the perfection of the moment, soaking in the heated gift from his body. A third, weaker shot, but oh, so hot from his body, dripped onto the hood of my clit.

Fuck. I loved the way it felt on my skin. That was what I lived for, the perfect contrast of my frigid clit and his hot cum. Blood raced through me. I could hear it pounding in my ears, and my heart, shocked into service, beat against my ribs. I was already throbbing inside.

Devon immediately climbed off the table. He pulled the bottom sheet down to my ankles. Hurrying, he stood by my head. Something he'd never done before, he bent down and placed a reverent kiss on my lips. I could smell his sweat on his neck. Then he gently pushed my eyelids closed, and I felt the sheet cover my face.

Immersed in darkness, electric halos slid across my vision. I didn't move. Everything was so perfect that I didn't dare breathe.

The door discreetly clicked shut.

I flung back the sheet and spread my slit to see the cum oozing there. My hand immediately moved to smear it across my clit in large circles. I furiously rubbed my sex back to life. The slick load clung in thick globs to my pubes.

So warm. Warmth is life.

Everything was perfect. Perfect, that time. Better than fantasies.

A spasm shot down my legs. I drew my knees up and spread my legs wide. Pinching and pulling, I overloaded my clit with sensation—hot cum, cold fingers. My hands made tighter circles.

Yes. Yes.

In the overhead mirror, I watched the cum trickle down to my hole, felt the slow, pendulous drop spread. Blood engorged my clit. The muscle hardened under my fingertips.

Fuck.

My lips pulsed.

My hand was almost a blur. Hard peaks hit short plateaus but built. My shoulders lifted off the table. Inside, my pussy clenched tight.

Perfect.

A furious orgasm more intense than any other shot though me.

God or the devil, it was fucking perfect.

I collapsed back onto the table. The headache started

almost immediately. I rolled on my side, gathered the sheet around me, and eased off the table.

My legs ached with every step. A cramp threatened my toes. Feeling years older, I opened the door to the bathroom.

By the time I hobbled down to the foyer, static vision made my left eye useless. Two fingers of whiskey, neat, and Vicodin only took the edge off. I wrapped my scarf tight around my throat.

Devon hailed a taxi for me, stepping out bravely into the onrush of night traffic while I waited under the awning. He opened the door and smiled at me as if I were simply a lady, and he, a gentleman. When I stepped off the curb, his hand was immediately at my elbow, but I stepped into a pothole of slush that splashed inside my black pumps anyway. Before he closed the door, I slipped the neatly folded bills into his hand.

"Thank you, Ma'am."

It was a hundred more than my usual tip, but he deserved it.

Christ, I was sore. Once the chill got into my muscles, it seemed to take days to coax warmth back into them.

I told the cabbie my address on Lakeshore Drive.

The headlights of oncoming traffic were like daggers in my brain, so I closed my eyes and tipped back my head. I exhaled.

Perfect.

No need to ever do it again.

I could go home and crawl in bed and shut out all the lights, sounds, feelings, and immerse myself in darkness. The pain would go away. My thick blankets would be so warm, and my sheets would be like silk on my skin. I could sleep sound, knowing that I had touched perfection.

The cold trickle of slush inside my shoe slid under my toes.

Except that he kissed me.

I rubbed my forehead, as if that could bring relief. The static in my vision slid to my right eye. I didn't want to vomit in the cab, but I felt the nausea rise. All I wanted was perfect black, without shade, without texture, without noise. I wanted the world on the other side of that darkness, far away, and warmth coating me like cum hot from a man's body.

Except that I felt the warmth of Devon's hands through his gloves. It would have been so much better if the only warmth I ever felt was his cum. That would be truly perfect.

I opened my eyes. Every streetlamp sent a prick of pain through my skull. My legs ached.

Heavier gloves. Maybe if he didn't touch me at all. Or maybe I could get him to chill his hand too. Of course I could. I paid for it, didn't I?

I pulled my coat around my neck and stared out at the black expanse of the lake as the cab traveled north. We drove and drove, but never seemed to get any closer to it.

THIS FLESH HAS CHANGED MEANING

Jennifer Cross

It's forever since we had sex. Okay, a couple months. Still, even that feels like an eternity for a couple who were regularly getting it on even right up through my last month of pregnancy: My clit, labia and breasts got so sensitive that I can hardly believe either of us got any work done. As soon as you walked in the door at night, I was all over you, pulling you into the bedroom or living room for further explorations of this unfathomably changed thing that was my body. And you—you couldn't get enough of me, hands wrapped constantly around the bulbous swelling that was the evidence of our soon-to-be son. Some women, they talk about working right up to birth, no bed rest. There was no bed *rest* for me, either. I was too busy getting busy.

You kept me up all night, inhabiting my inhabited body.

Of course, though he caused a very few hiccups in our sex life while still in the womb, now our routine is all shot to hell: If I'm not nursing, one of us is struggling to soothe or ease back into sleep our colicky child. My body feels like emptied baggage—a utensil that's served its purpose and been discarded. You soothe me, nights, with hands doused in arnica or geranium oil, and if we're blessed with a handful of minutes of silence, then we make use of it by sleeping rather than getting frisky.

When I met you, you came into my heart and body like an unfurled dream, and revealed all your passion and honest desire slowly, over time, as you figured I could stand it. And it turned out I could. I was intrigued with your idea of children and family—you, this big butch dyke who never considered giving birth yet wanted the fact of it, the work of home and hearth, the experience of delivering to a child what you never had for yourself. And over our own time, something lodged itself in my flesh: a desire, not unlike hunger, not unlike lust, to hold children—yours/mine/ours—in my body.

And now, what else could our bodies possibly mean? Our hearts pound in service of another. My breasts aren't for my pleasure alone anymore; they serve a purpose even I think of as greater (and I've been in the business of deifying every taboo in the pursuit of erotic joy)—the delivery of sustenance to a child. It feels almost unsafe to contemplate fucking: not bodily, really—all my birth wounds are healed. And today, again, I get the go-ahead from my doctor. Not just the go-ahead but the straight-out urging. "Get back into bed," she instructs me, desperately trying to get me fucking—that is, get me moving back toward my old routine. She thinks it would be good for my mental health and my mothering. But suddenly, or not so suddenly, really, everything's been destabilized. My sense of myself has gone through a revolutionary transformation, and it all feels too fragile to fuck with, so to speak: Now I'm a mother. Do mothers even *do* the kinds of things I did with you before this child was born of my body—things I was doing practically at the onset of labor?

After the ob/gyn appointment, I was out for another half hour, trying to write. But all I could do was stare at the people having conversations about something other than poop consistency and the pros and cons of booster shots.

When I get home, the baby is asleep, and you have your eyes closed, head laid back on the couch, with unfolded laundry—onesies and spit-up napkins and diapers—spread across your lap, on the couch, on the floor at your feet. It's late afternoon, and the evening light has begun to cast a yellow shadow across the room, heating everything up. The light feels thick, tangible, somehow slowed. I just want to sit and watch you for a while, share this quiet space, the sunset, the peace. But the laundry needs to get put away, and anyway there's dinner to make and lord knows the baby won't sleep long—he'll be hungry, too.

I reach down for the diaper in your hand. The room smells of the child's skin, of our desperate terror and horrific wondrous love, of milk and laundry soap and fabric softener. You open your eyes when you feel me tug at the cloth. But before I can get anything folded, you ease me off balance, bring me into your lap, and, smoothing my bangs away from the corner of my mouth with your sun-warmed hands, pull me to you with both of your hands—those strong appendages that once just seemed the instruments of my pleasure, but now I have seen them cradle my child, our child, at the moment of his birth, and I know they are so much more.

You pull me to you with hands so gentle they were able to soothe a terrified child's entry into this new atmosphere, this existence—those hands that seem to be meant now only for a tiny person's well-being. You soothe them strong across my shoulders, gripping my face and pulling me in for a kiss, eyes searching mine wonderingly, wondrously. We cannot speak, because there's no language for this moment. You press your lips meant for the top of a child's head to my lips meant now also for the top of a child's head, and we are kissing, eyes closed after affirming one another's deep need.

My hands, meant to cradle a nursing infant, meant to bathe, to count fingers, to wipe clean, are soft on your cheek, are tangled in the soft naps of your hair, and we are lovers now again, my body transitioning back. My cunt, which last shuddered so after releasing the child's placenta, begins to swell and pulse. This flesh has changed meaning, become a different sort of portal, become the thing that allowed this new life.

Now I inhabit the varieties, the multiplicities of being, cradled by you here on this couch, surrounded by baby infant things, dykes reduced or held up to motherhood. Your hands transmit their magic to my thighs, hard and fast, so immediate, the longing fast and urgent, and I rotate myself around, quiet, the child still sleeping—a miracle. My legs split and straddle the berth of your lap that's become a cradle. I lean down, press hot lips to yours, my hair falling against your cheeks and neck. You urge me up, help me up slightly, and release from the confines of your jeans your preparation for my return home.

I wonder if you worked extra hard to get him to sleep. It doesn't matter. I've got a skirt on, miracle of miracles (I forget how you suggested it), and you slide your cock against, then move aside, utilitarian panties. You feel the promise there for you, feel the glistening juice, feel the body of me aching for the body of you. We barely gasp, struggling to share ourselves in silence. I realize we will need to get a babysitter for ourselves soon, a night off, a night for noise and need. For now, it's minutes that we've got, maybe, and I bury my face in your shoulder while you bury your cock slow and gentle, careful, so unlike the usual, that immediate and hard thrust to meet my need. Your delicacy brings out the tears, and then we aren't coming but fucking, yes, fucking hard against each other, into our selves.

I gasp when you stroke my nipple, and the child shifts. We freeze, but he doesn't wake up. Our time is cut short, we know, and you grip me hard to your hip, tongue wrapping around one still over-sized nipple, reminding me of what these breasts used to be for. You grind into me, against me, while I, hand shoved down between us, stroke my clit fast and faster. I have to bite down when I come, and it's you who groans, finally, just too loud. The child, across the hall, whimpers. I continue to shudder and lean against you, whimpering myself, recovering, while you whisper your love in my ear. I press myself against you, your body fully under my body, for as much of this adult-to-adult, lover-to-lover contact as I can get before the rebirth, reemergence of our motherhood.

HANDS

Jean Casse

He was the most girly guy I'd ever made love to.

"Lick my big clit," he said, holding his pink cock to my lips.

It was a full seven inches, the exact distance between my thumb and forefinger, but it was small compared to the long-fingered hand that held it, a smooth, well-manicured hand so big it was almost scary. I wanted those fingers on my clit, up my cunt, in my ass; I wanted his hands to go everywhere they could possibly fit.

I thought he'd want me to close my mouth around his offering while giving those fingers a suck into the bargain, but the big clit deflated when he caught a glimpse of my tongue.

"What's that?" he gasped.

"It's a gold stud, like an earring. My tongue's

pierced," I explained. "Don't worry, it won't bite."

"I don't want anything hard on my clit. Take it off!"

"Easier said than done," I said. "I'll need my special mouth-wash to soak it in, I'll need to clean my tongue, the whole rigmarole."

My girlfriend, his lover, sat beside him on their couch, rubbing his shoulders. "It's just a smooth, round ball. I liked it!" she said. "Come on. Your clit's gonna love it."

"Tell you what," he said, "let's use hands tonight."

My clit throbbed at those words as I reached out for his, stoking it back to firmness, my mouth discreetly closed, because to me hands are the sexiest part of the body.

Of course, this didn't happen exactly the way I tell it, but that's why I write: It's easy to invent stories that tell the truth without the constriction of reality. Call them A and B, or Ann and Bill. I met her when she came in to get another piercing in her ear at this place where I work. I don't do the piercing; I wear white and sit in the reception area making appointments and taking money, because that's what girls do if they aren't really nurses.

Ann was as skinny as a twelve-year-old boy, with spiky-short dark hair, wearing faded jeans and a leather vest with the top two buttons undone. She leaned over my desk, revealing her breasts all the way to their tight, dark nipples, then clutched her vest together with perfect little hands, the nails bitten short. It was the sight of those hands that brought me to a lust so immediate I could almost feel her smooth fingers moving in my cunt.

"Do you want anything else pierced?" I asked, licking my lips to show her my tongue jewel. "Nipples, lips, thumbs?" My job was to sell the client more than she thought she wanted. Thumbs were my own fetish; nobody pierces their thumbs, though I always hope to find a fellow admirer of the hand who'd want a ring in that web between thumb and forefinger.

"I just do ears," she said, and in fact both her ears were studded all up and down with diamonds, emeralds, rubies, and rings. It didn't look like anything else would fit on there, but she wanted one more ring at the top of her left ear, saying it was a gift from her lover.

I was jealous. "What lover would want to hang more hardware on your poor ears?" I asked.

"My husband, actually," she said.

"Really?"

Husband was not a concept I'd associated with her. I thought maybe she meant lesbian husband.

"We're not married," she continued, "but we just moved in together, so he already feels like my partner for life."

"So this partner is of the...um...male persuasion?"

She gave me a surprised glance, then spread her hands out before me, palms up. "Yeah, he's a guy." She smiled, she held my eyes with hers, then stared into my open mouth. "I see you don't do ears," she said.

Which is true. Only my tongue is pierced.

It's a talent to be straight with men, slant with women, and rare to find someone else with the same ability. Talking with her, I sensed we both had the same desire for men, for women, and maybe even for hands. I took a check, even though I wasn't supposed to, and made a mental note of her address, which she had to write because she'd just moved.

It wasn't far from my place.

I wanted to hold her heart, to feel her pulse against my fist. She would be slow and easy as my fingers slipped through her rosy, moist lips, while her partner pressed his palm against my mound. It's hard to arrange an affair with a man and a woman at once. If they're strangers, there's awkwardness, and if they're lovers, there's the danger they'll pair off without you. I thought things might work out with her and her partner, giving me a chance to have four hands at once. I'd take his, sight unseen, because I trusted her to pick a fine pair.

I invited her for a drink after the piercing. "You'll need it," I told her as I led her to an examining room. "You're the last customer, so we'll be closing soon."

Her dark eyes were still fixed on my mouth, so I stuck my tongue out to give her another look.

She smiled. "Did that hurt?"

"It had a nice ache for awhile, but now it just feels normal." I smiled back.

A couple of hours later we were at my place, after drinks in a bar so noisy we couldn't hear to talk. Soon I led Ann to my bed.

"Oh," she said, her voice muffled in the pillows as she lay prone, her vest on my floor, her jeans half off, her cunt on my moving hand. "Oh, I should let Bill know I'll be late. We're open, we both have other lovers, but we agreed to always call to let each other know where we are."

"Maybe we could all get together sometime," I said, my heart jumping.

"Sure," she said, and then she was on me, unbuttoning my shirt, unzipping my jeans, her tongue and fingers everywhere at once, licking and flicking at my breasts and my clit, her hand creeping finger by finger into my cunt until her little fist was pumping in there, knocking against my womb, feeling so good I never wanted it to end. When I finally came, it felt like the whole world came with me.

I pushed my tongue into her mouth, clicking the stud against her teeth, then trailing it slowly down her breasts and belly to warm it in her cunt before applying it firmly to her clit as my fingers entered her. We were humming in unison, my mouth on her clit and my hand in her cunt until she cried out, shaking, "Don't stop," and I didn't until we both zoned out.

When I came out of my daze, she was up and wandering around my room, going through papers on my desk.

"Oh," she said. "I guess we fell asleep. I didn't call Bill, and now it's midnight. I don't know if I should call or just go home."

"Spend the night," I said. Spend it, don't hold on to it, and don't waste it.

"We agreed not to do that unless we plan it a week in advance." She picked up one of the notebooks I kept stacked on my desk. "You keep a journal?" she asked.

"Put it down," I told her, because she was getting way too personal for someone who wasn't even going to stay the night.

She flipped through the pages, too fast to be reading. "Will you write about me?"

"No. I make stuff up. Those aren't journals, they're stories."

"Well, are you gonna make stuff up about me?" She put down the notebook and grinned.

"Of course," I answered, sticking out my pierced tongue.

Her nipples stood up in the streetlight coming in through

the window, reaching for it like seedlings seeking sun. That got me out of bed to stand behind her and cup her breasts, so small they scarcely filled my hands.

"Stay," I whispered into her feathery hair.

But she left that night, and every night for weeks.

"Bill and I discussed you, and we decided no overnights for a while," she told me. "I told him you might want to hook up with both of us, but he says he's not ready."

I knew she was telling him everything, just as I wove everything into stories, so I worked hard to give us both plenty to say. *My hand was up her cunt, holding her pulsing womb as she came, juice sliding down my wrist....* I was writing the passion I hoped she was relaying to Bill.

When I asked again about meeting Bill, she said, "Not yet. He's feeling a bit insecure about us."

I hoped he was.

Then one day she said it was time.

"After what he's heard, of course he can't wait." I nudged her. "Does he like fists, too?" My fingers were hot for his ass.

"He's not into that," she said. "He just likes doing cunts."

My arms were going all goose-pimply wondering what his hands were like. I was even starting to want his cock, or maybe just what it represented: better jobs, more money. Bill was a computer consultant, part-time work that gave them plenty to live on, which meant that Ann didn't have to work. She could take classes, keep house, have lovers, or do whatever she desired with her time. I wanted to share that easy life. I began to imagine that Bill might enjoy two partners, one who looked like a cute punk twelve-year-old boy, and the other me, a deliciously plump blonde who was Ann's physical opposite.

When we met, I saw that Bill was both wage earner and wife. He cooked dinner; when I put a wineglass on the coffee table, he whipped out some coasters with Van Gogh paintings on them; he did the dishes while Ann and I necked in the living room on a beige tweed couch that matched the two chairs on either side of the flagstone fireplace. Their flat was so perfect it made me nervous.

"We don't have to hide," she said, when my acute hearing picked up his steps tiptoeing down the hall. "Bill knows everything."

We unzipped each other's pants.

So there we were on the couch, with Bill between us. Ann took the lead, placing one of his beautiful hands on each of our knees. I put my hand over his, tracing the thick, short-nailed fingers while getting so wet I was afraid I'd stain the upholstery. Then he took off his pants and presented me with that big clit. When my tongue jewel put him off, I stuck a finger in my mouth, then ran it around his cock head. Clit head. Whatever.

"A little to the left," he said. "Ahhhh..."

He was a big man, over six feet tall, with shoulder-length brown curls on his head, and soft brown hair on his arms and chest. With his tender voice and gentle hands, I kept imagining him as the largest, most substantial (although flat-chested, hairy, and huge-clitted) woman I'd ever met.

Ann brought out some Astroglide, which she squirted as needed while I rubbed him until my hand was about numb. Bill reached around to stick a couple of fingers in me, apologizing because his hands were too big to fist me. He was right; those two fingers were plenty. His thumb on my clit felt like the palm of a hand, but I could hold on, and then I couldn't; I came in a flash, like a lightbulb exploding.

"That's okay," he said, rubbing my back after I collapsed on top of him. "We'll teach you to last longer so it'll be much more intense for you next time."

Now, I typically take a while to come, so speed was something new that I wanted to try again, right away. "I've never been this quick," I told him. "I like it."

"I can take his whole fist," Ann bragged.

His cock was still swollen, but he pushed my eager hand away. Ann lay down before us and spread her legs, flashing the pretty pink clit hidden by her swollen lips. I felt my fingers twitch as if they wanted to be down in there, but Bill's big hand blocked the way, just about covering her whole pelvis. I watched his long fingers slip in one by one until, with a grunt, she took the whole thing. I thought I could see that hand moving in her belly, thumping up and down while she moaned, crying "Don't stop, don't stop" for what felt like hours until, when she came, his hand popped out like a champagne cork.

I'd been sitting on my knees so long they didn't feel like part of my body anymore. His hand looked misshapen, like the head of a newborn baby. Ann lay between us, so pale and sweaty I was afraid to look at her cunt.

"She's the only woman I know who can take me," Bill said with pride, flexing his hand. "It takes time to build up to it." He eyed me.

"Don't you want to go first?" I asked. I wanted that hand for sure, but I thought I might not be able to take it the first time, and I hate failure.

"I'm fine," he said, his cock now relaxed. "My pleasure is giving pleasure."

I felt funny, because I'd had occasion to use that line with guys, so I gave him a knowing look, woman to woman, as it were.

He just said, "I think we should wait. It's late and I have to see a client early tomorrow morning. Let's get together next week."

I practiced stretching my cunt, first with my own hand, which wasn't nearly as big as some I'd had, then with the head of a doll that was supposed to be the size of a real baby. No problem. I figured I was ready. Before I went over to their house, I rinsed my mouth well with Binaca and hot water, took out my stud, and left it to soak in a dish on the bathroom sink. Since Bill hadn't come last time, I was determined to get that big clit in my mouth before he put his hand in me.

Bill made crab bisque for dinner, and I rolled my naked tongue around my soup spoon to show it off, but he didn't notice.

"He seems moody tonight," I said to Ann when he left the table to make coffee.

"He gets like that," she said. "Must be his period."

"His what?"

"Men have hormones," she sniffed. "Their moods shift with the tides. If you'd ever been with one for long, you'd know."

Meanwhile, I could hear Bill whistling in the kitchen. Maybe he was schizoid, like this cat my mother used to have. When you'd stroke him, he'd purr and go all misty-eyed, then leap up and scratch your face. You never knew where you were with that cat.

When he brought the coffee back to the table, Bill was silent again.

"Did you turn on the heat in the bedroom?" Ann asked.

"Of course," he sighed.

I was afraid he was about to scratch, but I've always liked the excitement of a possible bite-back, that hint of something psycho. I loved my mother's cat. I ran down the drafty hall with them and jumped on the bed.

"Do you want to get out the ties?" he asked Ann, who went to the chest and opened the bottom drawer.

"Hey," I said to him, "aren't you going to let me suck your big clit first? I owe you."

"Maybe later," he said.

Ann was pulling out actual neckties in a variety of colors and designs. She took a fistful and dumped them on the bed. Bill sorted through them, his long fingers stroking the silk, the wool, holding them up to the light, rejecting one pattern after another until he found a light-blue paisley he liked. He asked us to take our clothes off and sit on the bed, back to back, while he bound our wrists together with that tie. He stood beside the bed, waiting, I supposed, for Ann to tell him what to do, but she said nothing.

He knelt on the bed beside us, putting a hand on each of our cunts, fingering us together. Ann sighed and leaned into my back, lifting her legs to let him in. I kept my knees together so that he had to work to insert just one finger, which was all I was going to allow until he let me suck him. But he wasn't putting his hand up Ann, either; this was just clit action, and she came quickly, which made him cluck with annoyance. I felt that I might not come, because what I really wanted was his whole hand, so I thought I'd fake it after a suitable length of time. I moaned, I shivered, and then my knees relaxed and opened in spite of themselves while his cocklike finger moved in and out through my flowing juices. When Ann reached around to press on my belly, that did it; I came for real.

"Better," he said, in a tone only slightly less than approving, as he untied us. "And now," he announced, "I'm ready to take your tongue stud."

Oh. I stuck out my tongue. "Sorry," I mumbled, rolling my tongue outside my mouth.

"What have you done!" he cried.

Ann looked, too. "You took it out?" she asked. "After all the trouble I had getting Bill psyched up to take it?"

"I left it at home. I'll wear it next time," I promised.

"No," said Bill. "You're going to wear it now. We're going to your place. Ann, go get the car."

I was right: schizoid. We pulled on our jeans and did as he ordered. My pussy was pulsing with the aphrodisiac of his demands. If I obeyed him, I was sure he'd let me suck his clit *and* take his fist.

My place was one room, with a small stove and sink in one corner, a bed and a desk in the other. The bathroom so full of sink, shower, and toilet a small person couldn't turn around in it. Bill had to pee. We could hear his elbows bump against the walls, and then a crash, which I knew was the glass of Binaca with my jewel in it hitting the tile floor.

"Dammit!" Bill yelled.

The bathroom door popped open to reveal Bill on his hands and knees, his head resting on the toilet, his giant fingers hovering across the floor feeling for the stud.

"Here, let me." I tried to pull him up, but he wouldn't budge.

"I've got it!" he said, holding up his thumb and forefinger.

"Put it in."

First I had to clean up the glass and the spilled Binaca, and fill another glass, clean off the stud, clean off my tongue.

"We're waiting," Bill called from the bed where he and Ann reclined, already nude.

"We'll start without you if you don't hurry."

"Some things can't be hurried," I explained, feeling an odd throb in my clit when I slipped the gold stud into its hole before shucking my clothes.

Ann and I laid Bill down between us and went to work. She tongued him first to get him warmed up, and then I put my hard jewel to the side of his cock, sliding it up and across the head.

"Smooth," he said.

"Told you," said Ann. "It feels real good on your clit, doesn't it?"

But what Bill had tonight was definitely a cock, and suddenly I wanted it pulsing inside me, and not just in my mouth. My cunt needed to be warmed up for his hand. I ran my stud down his shaft one last time, then lifted myself on top before he knew what I was up to.

"Oh," Ann warned me, "he doesn't like that."

"Not very girl, is it?" I said as I rode him, holding him tight between my knees. He was certainly strong enough to have thrown me off if he'd wanted to, but he didn't.

Ann sat back to watch while he growled beneath me, a giant bear grumbling his arrival, coming, coming, and there he was, bear whiz overflowing.

Lots of it, as if he hadn't come in months, years, maybe never.

"What have you done to him?" I asked Ann.

She shrugged. "He told me he didn't need anything more than to satisfy me," she said.

No wonder he was moody. "You can't believe what men say," I told her.

Bill snorted, which I thought was a sign he agreed with me, but then I realized it was the beginning of a snore, huge, rumbling, eternal. Ann and I wouldn't sleep that night, but we didn't care as we gently played with each other.

"He'll wake up," I told her, sliding my fist up her cunt. "And when he does, you'll be ready. His cock is almost as big as my hand." Suddenly I realized how much *I* wanted his giant ham of a fist up me. Bill snored soundly, hands limp at his sides. I'd cheated myself out of them.

Ann and I must have fallen asleep, too, because when I woke up, Bill's curly head was hovering over me, his soft lips on my mouth.

"Hello," he whispered, sliding a hand between my legs. Ann snored gently beside us. I turned to her, but he murmured, "Let her sleep."

His hand was very wet, sticky, well-lubed. His fingers crept into me, one at a time, my juices flowing down to met each one. I was having him, I was taking him in, and soon I felt his whole, hard hand in me, filling me up as I'd never been filled before.

"I knew you could take me," he whispered. "You're bigger than Ann." I pillowed my head on his soft chest hair as he twisted that hand inside me, running his fingers over my cervix until I thought I'd scream. This time I held back, this time I knew when to grab his wrist to slow his hand, when to raise my hips to take him deeper, how to pull back from the edge of coming. I lasted long enough to impress him; I lasted beyond the need to scream as I came. When he pulled out his hand, my cum was pooled in his palm, so he let it drip on my face, feeding me my own sweet fishiness.

When I ride the bus to work, I look at hands, but never find any as good as Bill's or even Ann's. The women's nails are too long, too painted, and the men's hands are rough, the nails jagged and often dirty, the skin scaly. Even large hands seem unexciting because I can tell they're attached to people who haven't got a clue what to do with them.

Hands matter to me because they're the true sexual organs. You'd think we'd all be required to wear mittens or risk arrest for indecent exposure, but lucky for me, no one's on to this, so hands are left naked for the admiration of a few connoisseurs. It's the rare person who knows about hands, but I keep searching. Not that I'd want to replace Ann and Bill, but a woman can't have too many available hands, which is why I'm always on the lookout for that perfect size, that long-fingered, short-nailed smooth sexual organ. If you see me, just wink so I'll know you know what I know.

COWBOY

Rita Rollins

I'm in the forest and I'm getting nailed up
against a tree—no, I'm at the beach, lying
down in the sand. The grains of sand are
massaging my back as a man's rough hand
is touching my smooth legs, and…where did
his hand go? Maybe it's a woman. Yeah, a
beautiful woman, the woman of my dreams,
she is rubbing my leg. She moves her hand up
my thigh—oh, no…the beach could be cold or
rainy or windy, it's…impractical. Start over.
We're in a hotel room. Okay, that's nice. It's
a nice hotel room with clean satin sheets, and
we've just finished off some champagne. The
woman of my dreams starts to lick between
my legs. A man comes up to deliver more
champagne. He watches her eating me. He
drops the champagne. He unzips his pants,

and we both want to suck him off at the same time. But we want to tease him first. I take off his tie so I can use it to bind his hands together. I shut the door.

I come, and I'm all alone, the fantasy left unfinished. I want to know who these dream people are, when they will come and release me. But now it's getting late, and I have to go to work.

I venture out onto the busy Friday-night sidewalk, past the jazz clubs and pizzerias, and I stop at the address, 1313 Rochester. It's my home away from home. It's where I go to help other people dream. The red and black lights inside the club create perfect, inexpensive angels. Twenty dollars is all you need to get a private dance. I slide past the dancers and into the dressing room. I drop my light suitcase on the table and prepare to primp. Who will I be tonight?

Sometimes I am dark: dark hair, dark eyes, dark clothing. I am here to punish you. Sometimes I am light: blonde, amused, innocent. I am here to serve you. Sometimes I am here to indulge myself, and I put on fishnets with seams, and clothes that have tassels on them, and I dance to swing and pretend I am from a simpler time. You can watch if you want to, if that's what does it for you. Sometimes I barely dance: I just roll around the stage, grind myself against the pole; fuck my image in the mirror. My small pale breasts are reflected back at me. I watch my long, toned dancer's legs move. I see my dark-chocolate hair tangling and tumbling down my shoulders. My gray eyes are always smiling cruelly, as if I've got a secret. I cast a brief glance over my shoulder to look at a customer. I smirk and romance my own image again. Some men are most enticed when you ignore them. They can fill in the blanks; fantasize about me however they want to. I never involve myself too completely. That's the first rule of stripping.

I am surrounded by them now, as I dance and they watch. I am surrounded, but I am alone. I am a fish and they are outside the bowl.

I try not to feel so lonely. It's bad for business. I put on a cute smile and bat my eyelashes like a naive kitten. Here I am: I'm all yours. Dollar bills line the stage, and I think about my next shopping spree. That always cheers me up. A man at the end of the rack is watching me intently under the rim of his cowboy hat. He seems to be signaling me with his inky green eyes. He is as handsome as a real cowboy. I saunter over to him.

"What's your name?" he asks.

"Nico," I purr.

"Your real name," he says, with mock exasperation. His eyes have a friendly twinkle in them.

I giggle. "Not believable enough?"

He shakes his head. My eyes trace his face and land on his square jawline. His face is chiseled, and freckled with stubble along the edges.

"It's Rose," I say in all honesty. I don't know why I've surrendered my secret to this man with the wry smile.

"I like it. Rose," he says, tasting my name like candy. His lips look full and soft. They are a rosy pink and seem at odds with his masculine physique. I am seduced by the way he licks them slightly, bites them. I am all his. "Care to dance?" he asks.

"You want a show?"

"No," he says, stubbing out his Marlboro in an ashtray. "I want to dance with you."

"I can't," I explain. "It's against policy."

"I see." He looks around at the bodyguards and security cameras. "Well, how about a show, then?"

I lead him to the VIP area and show him to his seat. This room is even darker than the main room. Only our eyes are bright white. "Tell me a story," he suggests as I stand before him, lifting my skirt.

"I can't," I begin.

"Is that against policy, too?" he asks.

"No, it's just...I'm not very creative," I say, fingering one of my nipples softly through my shirt.

"Tell me what you would do to me, if, you know, it was allowed," he instructs.

"Well...I could try, but I'm going to have to charge you extra for that," I say nicely.

Without another word, he whips a hundred-dollar bill out of his pocket.

"Are you sure? That's an awful lot of money to pay for something that isn't even the real thing," I warn him.

He stares into my eyes, and says, "I just have this feeling about you. I know what I want."

Now I feel slightly under pressure, but I stumble into it anyway. "I would start by taking off your shirt, licking your chest."

"That's good," he whispers.

"I would lick all the way down to your waist, and would kiss every inch of skin above your pants." I pull down my top and rub my breasts as I continue. "Your hands would desperately try to push my head down, yet you would try to be as gentle as possible, and I would fight you. I would continue to tease you."

"You are a bad girl, aren't you?" he says with a chuckle.

"Yes, I am." I move a few inches closer to him, but I can hardly dance now. I am too excited, too caught up in the story. "Finally I would unzip your pants. I would take your cock out and rub it all over my skin. I would blow on it and lick it softly. I would make you want a blow job more than you have ever wanted one in your whole life."

He moaned softly, and I was amazed at my ability to draw him in. He was being a perfect gentleman otherwise. His hands were at his sides, and his cock was in his pants. It was only my voice and my story that brought him his pleasure.

"I would take you into my mouth suddenly, and completely. I'd take you in so deep that I could feel you in the back of my throat. I would slide my lips up and down your shaft, slowly but firmly. Just before you're about to come, I would pull away and stare up at you. Then I would stand up and push you over onto the bed. I would lift my body slightly over yours, and put my pussy on your lips. I would tell you to lick me, and you would lick my clit hungrily."

He smiles, and lets out a deep sigh, and it's enough to drive me crazy.

"I would try to restrain myself, but I would eventually just begin grinding my cunt into your face. You'd slap my ass for being so bad. I would continue to be bad anyway. You would go on spanking me. Finally, I would come all over your mouth.

"For the finale, I would sit down on your lap and slowly begin to fuck you. I would stay still for a moment, once you were inside me, so we could linger in that first moment where our bodies feel that ultimate pleasure. Then I'd move swiftly up and down your shaft, fucking you hard without warning."

I drop my skirt and continue.

"You would tire of my games and pick me up, push me over the bed and start fucking me from behind. I would feel you so much better that way. I would lose control and you would fuck me hard, holding my hair with your hand, pulling it a little bit. You would let me come, and then pull out just in time to spill yours all over my back."

Beads of sweat are on both our faces. We stare at each other for a moment, not wanting to break the spell. Finally he stands up and hands me the bills he owes me. "Thank you, Rose," he says kindly. "You made my night." He tips his hat at me warmly and smiles as he heads for the door.

I smile back and then close my eyes. I try to burn his smile and his cowboy hat into my memory. I try to hold on to his sea-green eyes and muscular body. I tuck his money into one of my stockings and gather up the rest of my clothes, very pleased with tonight. It's not just the money. I have a new story, to be used whenever I see fit. And now the blurry man in my fantasies will have defined features and character. And a cowboy hat.

RHYTHM LIKE A HEARTBEAT

Sophie Mouette

"Jason," Dee said, "is an ass. Good riddance to him."

We were walking down State Street. The cherry trees were blooming, filling the air with the scent of spring. Dee had already stopped wearing her winter coat and heavy sweaters, but I wasn't quite ready to reveal my body to the hated, coming summer. The body that Jason had quite clearly, quite cruelly, called fat when he left me.

When I didn't respond, Dee stopped and took my arm, not unkindly, but firmly, in that way that made it hard to argue with her.

"You know you're better off without him, right, Kayla? Because you're not fat." Before I could snort and point to my flab, she cut me off. "You're gorgeous and curvy. You'll never be heroin-chic thin, and I can't imagine that you'd want to. What I wouldn't give for lush hips like yours! They'd make dance class so much easier than it is with my little-boy body."

She started walking again, and I had no choice but to follow, puffing a little to keep up.

"Which reminds me," she said. "I'm taking you to dance class tomorrow."

"Not on your life!" I protested. But, dammit, she still had her hand on my arm. That's what you get for knowing someone more than half your life. You end up having to listen to them.

"You need the girl time," Dee said. "And it's fun."

"It's exercise," I corrected. "I'm allergic to exercise."

"It's fun," Dee repeated. "It doesn't feel like exercise. Remember when we used to go clubbing in college? It feels like that—just moving with the music."

I grunted to indicate my lack of belief. Clubbing didn't involve learning steps, or facing large mirrors. Besides, it was easier to flail around to a pounding beat after a couple of Cosmopolitans.

But it was Dee, and I would humor her. Come to a class or two, then fade back from them. I wouldn't lie (I couldn't lie to Dee), but I could work late a few times, get behind on the classes, that sort of thing.

I went to the first class expecting it to be hard. For the first twenty minutes or so, my brain felt overwhelmed by all the new terminology—shimmy, hip drop, isolation, camel—and my body felt overwhelmed trying to follow all the new movements. But soon I forgot about being overwhelmed. I was concentrating, yes, but I wasn't concentrating on how bad I looked. I was concentrating on getting this movement right, on that turning when the music called for it.

The teacher, Ginny, was good—I'll gladly give her the credit. Experienced as she was, she knew how to patiently lead a bunch of wobbly, uncoordinated newbies. And not one of us did anything perfectly the first time, so I didn't feel like a complete lout. She also had a knack for spotting the one thing each of us did really well and making sure we heard her compliment it.

"Kayla, you've really got that hip pop down!" she said. "You've got the perfect figure for that movement. It took me months to look that good."

Hey, maybe my big hips were good for something besides bumping doors open.

Ginny wasn't utterly skinny, either, which made me less self-conscious. Oh, she had toned arms and grace to die for, but she had a poochy little tummy that she didn't bother to hide. Instead, she wore a tight-cropped top and a flowing skirt that tucked under the soft flesh, exposing it.

Yet, when she did one of those amazing ab rolls, I could see the muscles moving beneath the softness that nothing short of liposuction could have done away with, and it was all incredibly sensual.

"I've seen rail-thin women do this well," Dee confided to me. "But if anything, they have to work harder."

As if to prove this, the skinniest woman in the class, a young thing with the blonde, tanned look of a surfer and a pierced navel that called attention to her ripped abs, was the first one to quit.

Dee was both right and wrong about it not being exercise. The dance studio would get hot and sticky, and "sweating like a pig" was, I felt, an apt description for the way I felt after class. And oh, the day after the first class, I thought I'd never be able to get out of bed—my legs and arms and tummy and everywhere else felt as if I was being tortured with hot pokers when I so much as breathed.

At the same time, though, it *was* fun. Like aerobics, but with a greater purpose. The first time I went through a series of steps without actually thinking about them, I felt giddy from the rush of success. Muscle memory, whatever, I didn't care; it just made me happy.

In truth, whether or not Cosmopolitans were actually involved, I'd always liked to dance. My parents have a hideously embarrassing home movie of me at age eight, my hair fluffed out like Madonna in her fluffiest phase and god-awful turquoise leg warmers around my ankles, twirling around the living room to Debbie Gibson. Jennifer Beals I wasn't (and never would be), but I liked the way music encouraged my body to move, even if I had to threaten my parents upon pain of death never to show those movies.

Music. Bottom line, music is what changed everything about belly dance class for me.

The first few weeks, Ginny used a CD player for musical accompaniment. It was easier that way, apparently, to pick the right beat for whatever our newbie bodies were badly attempting to pull off. It also meant live musicians wouldn't be bored out of their gourds, playing the same two bars of music over and over for a bunch of very confused women. But once we started to get used to the whole idea, once we started to be able to follow instructions and dance reasonably past two bars of music, Ginny brought in the musicians.

My first impulse was to run.

It was one thing to wriggle about looking like a fool with a bunch of women looking just as foolish. It was quite another to do it in front of trained musicians who knew what the moves were *supposed* to look like.

Musicians who included men. Damn it.

I'd gone from hiding at the back of class to easing my way toward the front. (So I could see myself in the mirror—yes, I was actually willing to look at my dumpy body because I found myself actually caring about whether I was doing the movements right.) Now I was forced to scuttle back a row in an attempt to hide myself in the group.

The men wouldn't be looking at me anyway, right?

That, however, didn't stop me from looking at them. Jason's callousness notwithstanding, I had a healthy appreciation for men, especially sexy ones.

And, oh, one of the drummers was really yummy.

Sandor reminded me a little of Naveen Andrews, the actor who plays Sayid on *Lost:* the swarthy smooth skin, the close-cropped beard and mustache, the black curly hair that he wore loose to his shoulders. He was slender, but muscles played beneath his skin as he played, and his hands were a practiced blur over the drum.

I'm ashamed to admit that once or twice I forgot to pay attention to my dancing because I was staring at him and quietly drooling.

I was getting wet in another place, too.

For the viewer, it's obvious how belly dancing is sexy. It's less obvious how it's sensual for the dancer herself. There's something about the rhythms that crawl under your skin, beat with your blood, the way good sex gets your heart beating. The motions are designed to entice, but they're also incredibly empowering. The dancer is the one who's in control. The dancer is the one who, just by the placement of her hands, says *Look at me*.

Saying *Look at me* was not something I was comfortable doing in real life. Even before Jason had performed the slam dunk on my ego, I'd been a little shy, a little self-conscious about the weight I'd put on in recent years. The more I danced, though, the more I understood how to say *Look at me*. I had a persona when I danced. When I danced, I wasn't just pudgy Kayla the media relations director. I was a dancer. A dancer whose movements suggested all manner of sensual pleasure—on her own terms.

Spring danced into summer to the music of oud and mizmar. So far, I'd missed only one class. (I really did have to work late that night.) Dee had been right: Belly dancing was addictive. The rhythms, the movements, the melodies. I found myself humming in the shower, doing hip drops while waiting in line at the grocery store, spending far too much money on CDs of Arabic music.

I knew dancing had become an obsession when I went to the studio on a non–class night to practice a particularly difficult move I was trying to master, a combination that merged a three-point turn, a series of hip drops, and a little chest pop that looked adorable when Ginny did it but just wasn't working for me.

I wasn't quite up to wearing just a little bra, sparkly beads or no, but compromised on a choli, a more covering crop top, along with baggy emerald-green harem pants. It left my midriff bared. I was slowly getting used to that. I had started to see a little definition in my abs, even. My hips, alas, remained stubbornly chubby, but now I did wear a fringed scarf around them so I could better see if I was doing the movements correctly.

I'd cleared it with Ginny that another instructor wouldn't be using the room that night. So when I walked in, I expected to be alone with the mirror. I absolutely didn't expect to find Sandor there, his drums already set up.

He smiled, dazzlingly white against his caramel-colored skin. "Good evening, Kayla. I'm surprised to see you— pleased, but surprised." His dark eyes sparkled as if he really was happy to see me and not just being polite.

To say I was flustered would be an understatement. "I thought…Ginny had said no one used the studio tonight. I thought I could…" My voice trailed off. "…practice?" I managed to squeak.

"I as well. My roommate is a law student and he needed quiet tonight to study so I cannot drum at home." I'd never heard Sandor talk that much in class and his voice, deep and honeyed, fascinated me. His English was almost too perfect, with the formality of someone who'd learned it in school in a country where formality still mattered. The slight accent he retained was charming.

"Well, I'll just leave you to it." My voice was squeaking again, worse than before.

He laughed. "Nonsense! I drum so women can dance to my music. Why shouldn't we practice together?"

Why not? I could think of all kinds of reasons, starting with the fact that he was a professional musician and I was a rank beginner, and ending with the fact that I had wasted a few pleasant hours over the past month masturbating to thoughts of him. But I wasn't about to tell him the latter, and when I tried the "I'm not worthy" angle, he just laughed again.

"Why do you think I play for Ginny's class? I like playing for new dancers and introducing them to the music I love so much."

At this I had to smile. "It's working on me. Middle Eastern music is so..." I hesitated. The word that came to mind was *passionate* but I couldn't get it out, not looking at Sandor, not remembering all the things I'd imagined doing with him. I settled on "so earthy and alive. Like a heartbeat."

"Then we will warm you up with an ayyoub. That is the one closest to the beating of a heart."

It was also one of the easiest for a beginner to follow, a simple 2/4, but he was kind enough not to mention that.

I stretched out briefly to a slow pulsing beat. At first, used to his presence in class, I was able to relax. But as I bent over to loosen up the backs of my legs, I swore I could feel Sandor staring at me, or more specifically, at my butt.

Probably in fascinated horror was my first, instinctive thought. I'd never checked the rear view of my poufy-pants–covered butt in this position, but it might be pretty appalling.

When I straightened up and glanced over at him, though, he didn't look especially appalled.

In fact, he gave me a flirtatious smile and a wink.

Probably he flirted with all the dancers he worked with, or for all I knew, with all women between age eighteen and the grave. Some men just flirted as naturally as they breathed. But that didn't stop me from grinning back at him and tilting my head in a way I'd picked up in class, a cute teasing gesture from Egyptian cabaret-style dance.

He picked up the pace of the drumming a little and I began

to dance, not trying the complex new move yet, but running through a series of basics: hip circles, hip lifts, chest lifts, and drops.

It felt very different doing it with his eyes on me. He watched sometimes in class, sure, but there were twelve of us plus Ginny to divide his attention, as well as interactions with the other musicians. The times I'd realized he was looking at me, it hadn't seemed personal.

Now it did.

The rhythm flowed out of his hands uninterrupted, but he never looked down. He never took his eyes off me. You'd think he actually found me worth watching, a real dancer giving a fabulous performance instead of a beginner running through exercises.

Finally, I stopped moving, put my hands on my hips and glared at him. "Cut it out!"

"Cut what out, Kayla?" To his credit, he made an attempt at looking innocent, which failed.

"Staring at me. It makes me self-conscious."

"How will you ever cope with an audience if one man unnerves you?"

I chuckled at the notion of me dancing at a nightclub in a body-baring, glittery costume, the way Ginny did.

Out of habit, I almost popped out with some self-deprecating remark about no one wanting to see a fat chick dance. But I didn't. For one, it would make me sound pathetic in front of a hot man, and that was no good.

For another, old habits or not, I wasn't feeling quite as self-deprecating as I used to. Between the dancing and the fact I was eating better without Jason's pizza-and-beer addiction to tempt me, I was now hourglass-shaped and moving toward fit instead of round and squishy. Sure, it was a larger hourglass than I hoped it someday might be, but what I saw in the mirror of late looked halfway decent even to my own overly critical eye.

The "dancing ladies" were helping with my new attitude as well. As I watched one of my new friends dance, I'd see some moment when the music moved her and she looked beautiful whether or not her body was spectacular.

If it was true for them, it must be true for me too.

And Sandor's flirting tonight was definitely helping me to believe it. It may be shallow, but it's true: Attention from a gorgeous man does boost the old self-esteem.

So I squashed the instinct to put myself down and said, "I'm not really interested in performing—I'm just having fun learning."

"I can tell. You light up when you dance, even just doing the drills. I love watching you—you look so beautiful."

"Sandor, you are *such* a sweet-talker! I've been dancing for nine weeks and still trip over my own feet half the time, my clothes clash tonight, and I've got a butt the size of all outdoors. But thank you."

"You need to see yourself through my eyes. Let me show you."

One of his drums had a carrying strap. He stood up and slung it across his body so he could play while moving around, as I'd seen him do for Ginny at a performance.

He moved behind me and broke into a strong, sensual rhythm. I couldn't conjure its name, but my hips remembered it and started twitching, swaying back and forth to the beat. At first I felt self-conscious, but the music was too inviting to resist. I raised my arms in my best approximation of the elegant curve Ginny taught us, corrected my posture, and let my hips do their thing, snapping and shimmying and circling as the spirit and the music moved me. My fringe swayed back and forth prettily—in time to Sandor's beat, I was pleased to realize. (I was still at the stage where that wasn't a given.)

"Look at your face, Kayla. See how joyful you look—how beautiful!"

Usually, when I danced in front of a mirror, I watched my form—or, despite my progress toward having something like self-esteem, zeroed in critically on my belly or my butt.

This time, I did as Sandor instructed and looked at my face.

Was that really me? I wasn't exactly a Hollywood vision. My hair was disheveled, and the makeup I'd put on before work was faded. But the smile, the rosy, healthy glow, the sparkle in my eyes—I really *did* look joyful.

And a lot closer to beautiful than I normally thought of myself. Maybe even sexy. It wasn't a word I usually associated with myself, but if I saw someone else looking as I did right now, I might think, She's pretty hot. Awful outfit, but pretty hot.

And with that in mind, I tried a move that Ginny had taught us a couple of weeks ago. I started shimmying my shoulders, then leaned back toward Sandor, still shimmying. I wasn't sure I was doing the move right, but it seemed to have the desired effect. That is, Sandor's reflection in the mirror grinned happily, and I felt sexier and more daring than I had in a long time.

"That's the attitude!" he said, and I basked in his approval.

He changed the rhythm to something a little slower and slinkier. At the same time, he angled to the side and leaned in toward me, so our bodies touched without the drum getting in the way. I liked that it was his side I was touching. It seemed safer, enticing without being slutty.

"Listen to my drum," he whispered. "It's telling you how beautiful you are." His voice was like honey, thick and sweet and flowing over me, a sensuous addition to the already alluring music. I could feel the heat from his body.

This was music for undulations and body waves, and that definitely fit the mood. I began a side-to-side undulation, torso first, the hips following.

"Habibi!" Sandor exclaimed, which, I'd learned, means something like "Oh, baby!" in Arabic.

And I looked in the mirror. Normally I didn't think this move looked good on me. But tonight something was different. I seemed more elongated, snakier, sexier. Practice had undoubtedly done its part to make things look smoother. But it was more that I finally had the right attitude. My face wasn't scrunched up with concentration. My body was relaxed, fluid. I looked like I was feeling sensual and having a good time.

It didn't hurt the fun-and-sensual aspect that I was undulating against Sandor. "Ginny had had us try it against a wall at first to help us learn not to twist," I said. "I should tell her doing it against a cute guy works better. I'm sure we could get volunteers."

"I'd happily volunteer, as long as I could work with you. I love watching you move, but feeling you move is even better."

My breath caught in my throat. I realized just how aroused I was. It had come over me while I was dancing. Now I became aware of the hard nipples pressing against the soft stretch velour of my choli, of the way all my blood seemed to be pooled in my pelvis, giving new weight to my movements, of the heat between my legs.

I glanced down. It was a little difficult to be sure, looking at an angle and around the drum, but it appeared that Sandor was enjoying himself just as much as I was.

We'd moved beyond casual flirting here into far more interesting territory. Sandor was still drumming and I was still dancing, but now it was definitely a mating ritual.

Sandor altered the drumbeat again, to something pulsating and distinctly sexual. It didn't sound like anything he'd ever played in class. It sounded as if he was pulling it out of somewhere, creating it just for me.

I danced a little while longer, letting the sound slip under my skin. Then I turned to face him. I wanted to kiss him, press myself against him, feel him hard against me. I wanted to do more than that: to liberate his cock, stroke it, suck it.

But even the new, more confident me wasn't ready to be that bold. So instead I moved to his music, undulating and shimmying so I was brushing against him half the time, closer than Ginny would have approved. (Or maybe she'd have applauded under the circumstances.)

And then I leaned in and kissed him quickly, a glancing, playful kiss that was far less than what I really wanted. That way, I figured, I could pretend it was all just silliness if I was misreading the whole situation.

He stopped drumming and tucked the drum around behind him. Then he put his arms around me and pulled me in for a real kiss.

By real, I mean I could feel areas inside my mouth that I'd never known were sensitive coming to life as his tongue flicked over them.

By real, I mean I temporarily lost higher brain function.

By real, I mean that by the time we came up for air, it was clear that we weren't stopping at a kiss.

"Does the door lock?" Sandor asked me, sounding as breathless and distracted as I felt.

"Shouldn't we…"

"We could, but not at my place. I promised my roommate a night of quiet, and I don't think this will be quiet."

I stunned myself by saying, "I hope not!"

"Besides, I like this room—all the mirrors. Have you ever watched yourself make love?"

Not likely. It had never come up until now, and if it had, I'd have found some lame excuse, or laughed nervously and changed the subject, or, most likely, fled in a panic. When you're at war with your body, the idea of watching yourself sounds more scary than sexy. My body and I were on much better terms now, but I was still not sure I was ready for that.

I must have looked anxious, because he shook his head slightly and pressed a finger to my lips. "No saying bad things about yourself, Kayla. You saw how beautiful you look when you dance. This will be even better."

I pondered this as best I could with a brain still melting from that spectacular kiss.

I trusted Sandor in this. Oh, he was pushing the sweet talk, as people do when they're hovering on the brink of tearing each other's clothes off. But when he'd shown me myself moved by dance and music, he'd shown me something of myself I didn't know. Maybe there was something to what he was saying. For that reason (and because I wanted him naked and touching me and didn't want to have to wait until we got to my place to do it), I said, "Sure. Why not?"

Sandor put his drum away while I locked the studio door. There were no other classes tonight, but it was possible that someone might have designs on practice space, as we'd had.

Another kiss, sweet and hot.

Sandor stroked the bare skin at my waist, bringing the skin to tingling life, then his hands glided around and across my belly. I felt that skin, too, catch fire—possibly the first time since I was a toddler that I'd taken pleasure in that part of my body. One finger circled my navel. I jumped at the sensation.

"Ticklish?"

"No, just surprised. It feels really good."

He did it again as if to make sure. It still felt good; shivery, but good. It seemed to connect to something deep inside my belly, to some of those underlying muscles I'd been learning to use in dance—ones that tightened up a bit as Sandor continued his explorations, reminding me that pelvic and abdominal muscles were useful for things besides dancing.

One hand continued to stroke my belly. The other snaked around, slipped inside the elastic waistband of my baggy, low-slung pants to cup my ass. He leaned in, kissed me again. I reached for him, grabbing at his buns, pulling him against me so I could feel his hard cock pressing against my belly.

The undressing started with my pants, before I was really expecting it. One second Sandor was playing around and through the acres of soft green gauze. The next, he'd pulled them down. I don't know if he meant to get the underpants or if they just went along for the ride, but once they were part of the fabric puddle at my ankles, the rest of our clothes were doomed.

Naked, Sandor was a caramel-colored treat, with just enough dark hair on his chest to give me something to pet.

Muscular legs matched the well-muscled arms I'd long since noted. There was a little softness at his waist, a homey touch that made the beautiful arms and legs and the sculpted shoulders more comfortable for a mere mortal like myself.

His cock was dark, purplish-brown, and jutted out at attention from a nest of black curls. "Nice," I breathed, and I weighed it in my hand. It felt dense, as if it was made of something heavier than human flesh. Putting two fingers on one side of it and my thumb on the other, I stroked up, circled the head with my palm, worked my way down again.

After a couple of months of being single (and a few before that when I might as well have been), I was a little surprised that my first burning interest was touching Sandor, rather than vice versa. But it made sense. I could keep myself supplied in orgasms, but I'd really missed another person, missed the fun of having a male body to explore and enjoy. I intended to have a lot of fun exploring Sandor's body—all of it—but I just couldn't resist starting with the cock.

Sandor caught my wrist after a few passes, just as a pearly drop of fluid peeked out from the head and I was considering whether to taste it yet.

"But I want—"

"And I want you to. But it's my turn first," he said, his voice soft but intense. "Turn around."

Maybe by going for his cock so directly, I'd been trying to avoid this moment of truth. I'd spent a lot of time in my life not taking good hard looks at my naked body in a mirror—at least not in any kind of friendly manner.

But Sandor's dusky coloring set off my ivory skin tone nicely, I had to admit, and the expression on my face, dreamy and sensual but tinged with heat, made up for any shortcomings I could find in my body. Like the dancer face, the foreplay face looked a lot better than my mental image of myself. Maybe I needed to update that mental image.

He cupped a breast with each hand, rolling my nipples between strong fingers, sending waves of sensation from my nipple to my sex.

"Look at yourself," Sandor whispered, nuzzling my ear. "You're flushed, starting to breathe harder. Your nipples are such a pretty color, such a lovely shade of pink, even pinker than your cheeks when you dance. See how they're crinkling up as I touch them."

Fascinated, I obeyed.

"I love your breasts. They're so lush and full and soft."

I'd have given him *full* before this moment, but my own impressions of them usually included complaints about their critical lack of perkiness. The way he held them, they looked much better: round, soft, voluptuous mounds like something out of a Victorian naughty picture. Maybe they looked more proportional in his long-fingered hands than in my own much smaller ones, or maybe it was the influence of the clever and delightful things he was doing to my nipples.

The stale-sweat smell of the studio seemed to fade and the flickering overhead lights weren't nearly as intense, so I was willing to believe that lust was having some kind of hallucinogenic effect, making everything prettier.

Then Sandor did something especially interesting—a little pinchy and twisty, but not painful, just intense—and I decided to shelve the whole thinking thing until much, much later. It seemed far more important to push back against him, feel his hard cock nestling into the crack of my ass.

Sandor worked on my nipples, occasionally whispering

words of encouragement, until I was cooing with pleasure and my pussy felt as if it was swimming in warm oil. Then he rested one hand on my belly, fingers pointing down. His thumb teased at the lower edge of my navel. The other fingers stroked at my mound, touching sensitive areas but not the most sensitive ones.

"Please—" I hadn't meant to beg, but he was so close to where I really wanted him that the word just slipped out.

"Not yet. I want you to feel where my hand is. This curve here, this little curve—it's beautiful when you dance, and it feels almost as good to my hand as your breasts do. It's womanly, and that makes it erotic." As he spoke, he was slowly stroking at my belly, while continuing to play with my nipple with his other hand.

I was on fire, twitching and bucking, making little pleading noises. I closed my eyes, but Sandor caught me in the mirror. "Look at yourself getting excited. It's so beautiful."

I opened my eyes, and what I saw was fascinating. My face was red and a little contorted. I wouldn't have called it beautiful at this point, but it was damn sexy, leaving no question what lustful thoughts I was contemplating. And my belly—my belly looked pretty good too, the way it was quivering under his touch. Even my hips, my dreaded wide load, looked more proportional to the rest of me than I remembered.

"You're right," I managed to say.

Then, and only then, did he reach down and drum gently on my clit until I came.

Somehow, I kept my eyes open for that, too. I saw it all— the crazy face, the blotchy flush on my throat and chest, the demented bucking. And that was beautiful, too, in its way.

Almost as beautiful as it was when we misappropriated a

couple of yoga mats from the corner to lie on. Sandor put me on top so I could get a good view, and I had to admit that we looked pretty damn hot together. Watching my ass move as I rode him gave me a new affection for that much-maligned part of my body. But after the first couple of minutes, I forgot to watch, too wrapped up in the beauty all around me.

The beauty was in his dark face and the way it showed the power I had over him in that moment, the way my body was affecting his.

The beauty was in how we moved together, and how I learned that the hip rolls and pelvic tilts I'd been practicing for dance class had very interesting effects on both of us when I did them with Sandor deep inside me.

The beauty was in how I felt as I shuddered around him, coming again with a violence that pitched me forward, too boneless to support myself anymore.

And in how Sandor rolled us both over, not with perfect grace, but with surprisingly little effort.

And in how he looked, lying over me, the muscles in his arms in tense relief as he pumped.

And in his expression just before he exploded in me. He came in Arabic, letting out a series of words that could have been endearments or curses or, for all I knew, the name of his last girlfriend. But it sounded to me like music, like the lyrics to one of the songs I was learning to dance to.

Exhausted, tangled together, I could feel the beating of our hearts, like the frantic drumbeats accompanying a whirling-dervish finale of dancing.

Ironically, I was on State Street again when it happened.

I saw Jason well before he saw me. Instinctively, despite

everything I'd learned about myself, I braced myself for his eyes to skim over me dismissively.

Well, fuck him, and the horse he rode in on. I added a little more sway to my step, realizing as I did so that I had already been walking that way, my hips moving sensuously. My head was thrown back, my spine straight. Somewhere along the line I'd stopped hunching over, trying to be invisible.

It was the height of summer, a season I'd formerly dreaded. Now, I wore a swirly patterned skirt that hit me just above the knees and a figure-hugging, ribbed red tank top. The sweltering heat had caused a shimmer of sweat between my breasts, and that was okay.

Still, what happened came as a surprise. Jason glanced at me—and didn't glance away. Instead, I saw him do to me what I'd watched him do to countless other women: His eyes fixated on my chest, took a long, slow vacation to my hips and down my legs, and then ambled back north again. A tiny smile quirked the left side of his mouth, and *he* stood up a little straighter as we neared each other.

Imagine that, Jason puffing himself up for me.

With what seemed like effort, he dragged his gaze from my chest to meet my eyes. A flirtatious grin started.

Then froze.

We both slowed. I could see the confusion in his eyes, then the sudden dawning.

"Kay—Kayla?"

"Hello, Jason," I said.

"I didn't recognize you," he said, sounding confused. "Have you changed your hair?"

"Something like that," I said, tilting my head in that flirtatious Egyptian cabaret move.

"Well, you...you look good. Really good."

"Thank you." I bit the inside of my cheek to keep from laughing. He scanned my body again, a small crease between his eyebrows as he tried to understand.

I had toned up, yes, but I was still a big girl. I'm sure he couldn't figure that out, what had changed, why I was suddenly attractive to him. Jason just wasn't the type to understand that attitude and confidence mean a lot more than zero percent body fat.

"Um," he said. "It's been a while. Would you like to grab a beer, catch up?"

"I'm sorry," I said, giving him my most dazzling smile. "I'm on my way to meet someone." It was Sandor's turn to have the apartment to himself.

As I sashayed away, I could see in the reflection of a shop window that he was still standing there, staring at my ass.

I couldn't wait to tell Dee.

PIVOT

Jane Black

I held my hair up off my neck as Keith buckled my collar—a little too tight for comfort,
as always. He turned me around to face him.
I was naked except for the collar, and he
stroked my nipples lightly. They liked that.
I leaned forward to kiss him but he stepped
back and said, "Later. There's something else
I want you to put on." He handed me a purple
rubber butterfly attached to a G-string. The
butterfly was a remote-controlled vibrator;
he'd showed it to me last week but I hadn't
tried it on yet.

I pulled the G-string over my thighs and
adjusted the butterfly to lie over my clit. I wondered whether it would actually feel like a butterfly, or more like a jackhammer. Though we
had lots of adult toys, perhaps surprisingly, I

didn't have any experience with vibrators. I tensed up, waiting for him to turn it on, but he didn't. He pocketed the remote and told me to get dressed.

I pulled on a black turtleneck sweater over the collar. Since both of our kids and the babysitter were in the house, discretion seemed prudent. Next came the skirt, hose, and fuck-me shoes. Keith had chosen what I'd wear, as he often does.

We said good-bye to the kids (who were slack-jawed, watching *Finding Nemo* for the buzillionth time) and got into the car to drive to the bar. While I was buckling my seatbelt, and before I even started the car, Keith switched on the vibrator. I jerked and said, "Shit!" and he laughed. I gave him a grumpy look, and struggled to get my seatbelt on. I felt as if I was going to jump out of my skin.

Initially the butterfly just annoyed me, buzzing against my shaved cunt and making me fidget. I knew Keith wanted me excited, but getting horny in public isn't easy for me. I get too distracted. And coming in public? I'd never tried it before, and it seemed unlikely—but I'd give it a shot. I wanted to please him.

We got to the bar and were seated at a table in a corner. Midway through our first martini, as Keith was saying something about fixing the roof of our house, I shifted in my chair and the thing buried itself deeper between my labia, pressing hard up against my clit. At that moment I lost track of what he was saying and my vision clouded. He noticed, smiled slightly, and watched me. A waitress showed up and said, "Two more drinks?" Keith nodded. I said nothing.

The restaurant was dimly lit and noisy. I stared off into the room, inwardly focusing my attention on my clit. Neither of us spoke. We must have looked as if we were on an awkward first date, making little eye contact and no conversation. The waitress brought us our drinks. Keith leaned forward in his chair, staring at my face, as he sipped his. I didn't touch mine.

We just sat there. As the minutes passed, I felt myself becoming slippery and throbbing. "Julia," Keith said softly, but I didn't respond. I willed him to stop talking to me. I wanted to come. For him. I spread my legs under the table, letting the vibrator in closer, letting it hum against me.

Time passed—five minutes? Ten?—and I began to feel the familiar sensation of being close to coming, like a ball in the final stages of circling down a funnel, making smaller and smaller concentric circles, speeding toward the center. I had begun breathing through my mouth and had my eyes half-closed and was about five seconds away from coming when Keith reached into his pocket and turned off the vibrator.

I startled. The room came into focus, hard. "Shit!" I said again, more loudly than I intended. The couple at the booth next to us looked over at me. Keith reached across the table and cupped my chin in his hand. "Just a reminder," he said softly, "that you're mine."

Damn it. As if I needed a reminder. As if I wasn't aware, every single day, of the immutable fact that I belonged to him. He could see it oozing from my pores, if he looked. I'd worked so damn hard to get horny, I'd almost come, and then he'd shut the wretched thing off just to make a point. I stared at him as he paid the check and stood up. I wasn't sure what was bothering me more, the intense sexual frustration or the feeling of being set up. As we left the bar, I felt a small, hard kernel of anger inside me. It was scraping—ever so lightly—against my love for him.

When we got home he paid the babysitter, walked her to

the door, then tied me to our bed and fucked me at length—
but no matter. I was too irritable and out of sorts to come. I
couldn't sleep afterward, and I lay in bed watching him for a
long time.

A week later, the babysitter was back, and the kids were in
jammies watching *Ice Age*. Keith and I were headed out the
door to dinner. I wasn't wearing my collar.

"My car or yours?" Keith asked.

"Let's take the minivan," I said, for a very good reason.
The minivan's deep, recessed floor bins are designed to hold
the rear seats when they're folded down, but they're also useful for storing other things. Soccer balls, for example. Grocery
bags. Sex toys.

Though minivans don't typically rate high in sex appeal, the
fact is that it's far easier to fuck someone in a minivan than
in, say, a Corvette. Corvettes may make you *feel* sexy, but if
you want to do anything about it, you'll have to go elsewhere.
Minivans, on the other hand, are total fuckmobiles.

"I'll drive," I said. Keith frowned, but tossed me the keys.

I drove to the neighborhood where the restaurant was, but
instead of parking in front, I headed down a dark, residential
side street and parked several blocks away. I turned off the
engine and sat there in the dark. Keith looked at me quizzi-
cally, his face half-shadowed in the moonlight.

I closed my eyes and summoned the residual kernel of anger.
I stroked it, focused on it. I meant to put it to good use.

"Get in the back," I said flatly. Keith started to say something but changed his mind. He moved into the back of the
van, where the back row bench was folded flat into the floor.
One of the two middle chairs was folded in half, making a

low table; the other was upright.

I was right behind him. I stopped in the middle of the van, and knelt by one of the floor bins. I took off the cover and pulled out a leather blindfold. I handed it to Keith, who was sitting cross-legged on the floor in the back, watching me. "Put it on," I hissed. He looked surprised, but took the blindfold. We'd occasionally switched roles before, but it had always been a game—even when I pretended to be in charge, we both knew otherwise. This time was different. I knew it. He knew it.

When his eyes were covered, I said, "Get undressed." He took off his shoes, socks, and shirt, and then awkwardly lay down and pulled off his pants and underwear. He sat up again when he was finished, his face completely serious now. I made him wait while I duct-taped pillowcases to the back windows. The windows are tinted, and nearly impossible to see into at night—but I didn't want to risk it.

I pulled him forward onto his knees and had him kneel over the folded car seat. I buckled leather wrist cuffs around both his wrists and snapped them onto the headrest. I sat back on my heels to look at him. In the shadows his body was lean and muscular. He was smooth and beautiful, as lovely as he'd been when we met nearly ten years ago. He wasn't hard, though, and he looked cold. Reflexively, I reached for the blanket I had brought, meaning to cover him, but I stopped myself. For the first time since we'd been together, I deliberately ignored his needs—as he had done mine.

It was a trivial act, by most measures. But with that choice, something larger shifted inside me, and the scene became more than a simple tit for tat.

For almost a decade the underpinning of our relationship

had been his dominance and my submission, both in bed and, to some degree, out of it. I dressed as he directed. I wore my hair long because he preferred it. If he woke up horny in the middle of the night, he would simply yank down my underwear, smear me with lube, and fuck me—often before I even woke up. In all ways, I belonged to him, I deferred to him. But in that moment in the minivan that sense of submission just...slipped off me. I did not belong to him. I was a free agent. A pissed-off free agent.

I went back to the floor bin and retrieved a harness and a small black dildo. I took off my skirt and underwear and strapped on the harness, positioning the dildo so that the base pressed against the bottom of my pubic bone. I grabbed a small bottle of lube. Kneeling behind Keith, I spread his ass wide open. I dripped lube down his crack and slowly pushed a slippery finger inside him. Though it wasn't the first time I'd fingered him there, it had been a while—he inhaled sharply and tensed up. I slid another finger in and began massaging his prostate. He arched his back and pressed back against my hand. I reached around with my other hand to his cock. He was rigid now, pulsing in my hand.

I stroked his dick while pressing my fingers deeper into his ass. His breathing became raspy. Slowly I withdrew my fingers—he grunted when the tips came out—and I pressed the tip of the dildo against his hole. I'd never done this to him before. He felt the silicone cock and I could see his ass cheeks clamp tight for a moment. Then he took a deep breath and relaxed them.

"Now I'm going to fuck you," I said, and I pressed my hips forward, easing the dildo inside. He didn't resist. I gripped his hips with both hands and began to fuck him. The base of the dildo pressed against my labia, and I could feel it in my clit. I was suddenly on fire with sexual desire. I fucked him hard but not too fast, careful not to rock the minivan. I ground my pelvis against his ass, feeling the dildo rub against me. He was moaning as he pressed backward with every stroke. In a few minutes I recognized his pre-coming sounds, and I immediately pulled out.

I unclipped his cuffs and pulled him up to a kneeling position. I took off his blindfold. Even in the soft moonlight he was squinting, his eyes already accustomed to full black. His erection jutted out from him, nearly vertical. He had a beautiful cock—long, slim, smooth, like cut marble. Perhaps I would have loved him as much if he were not so perfect, but perhaps not.

I lay down on my back, my knees bent and apart. He started to reach for me, but I said sharply, "Don't touch me! Just stay there." I spread myself open before him with one hand, and slid my fingers over my clit with the other. He watched me silently. I closed my eyes and rubbed hard and fast. I came quickly and then sat up. I pulled on my skirt. He looked surprised, and whispered, "Can I fuck you?"

"No. Jack yourself off," I said. So he did. He jacked himself off, kneeling in front of me in the back of the minivan. I grew hot again, watching his rhythmic strokes and seeing the semen bead up on the engorged tip of his penis. He ejaculated in a gush, splattering the blanket and the floor of the van and one of the rear cupholders.

He dressed himself slowly as I watched, and kissed my cheek when he finished. "I love you, Julia," he said, looking at me with an expression that I'd never seen before. "I love you, too," I answered.

I wasn't angry any more. I wasn't sure what I was instead.

We drove home silently, neither of us wanting to go to the restaurant. We cleaned up the van before going inside the house, and remembered to smile and be pleasant to the babysitter. We were briefly stumped when she asked how our dinner was, but Keith finally came through with "Um, it was good. I think. Yes." We ate leftover pizza in silence after she'd gone.

The next day we resumed our family life, and in most ways our lives were unchanged. But I thought of Keith constantly. I thought of him as I drove the kids to soccer games in the minivan. I thought of him when I was working, and found myself inconveniently wet and aroused, imagining him naked in the moonlight. As for Keith, he treated me more gently, and I would often catch him watching me as I bathed the kids or brushed my hair. Something had changed between us that night, and it didn't change back.

Marriage is a living, breathing thing. On unexpected points, it pivots. And then it becomes something entirely new.

FLUID HUMILIATION

Kayla Kuffs

"Buy an enema bulb," Jeff said.

I was somewhat taken aback. It wasn't really my kink—bathroom sports were not my idea of a good time. Though admittedly I had not had the experience, I just couldn't wrap my mind around going through it with any kind of dignity. I always considered it a limit. Now he wanted me to buy an enema bulb?

I sighed and tried to back my way out of it, but he was firm in his command.

"This is something that pleases me, baby, and you want to please me, don't you?"

He knew what buttons to push to get me to do pretty much anything, so of course I agreed to purchase the item. Just purchasing it was going to be traumatic.

In the pharmacy, I didn't really know

what I was looking for. An enema bulb—I shuddered at the thought. I wandered the aisles, trying to look nonchalant and inconspicuous. I casually stood before the personal hygiene section, my eyes running up and down the shelves trying to find the bulbs without letting other customers know what I was looking for. I was extremely embarrassed as I grabbed the enema bulb off the hook. Please, God, don't let anybody I know walk by me. I hustled myself to the cashier and almost threw the money at her. She was chatting away with another employee, not really paying much attention to me. Normally I'd be offended by that kind of behavior, but I was grateful for it this time. My purchase in the bag, I raced out of the store.

Later that week, my phone rang. It was Jeff. We talked a bit, and I told him I had purchased the bulb. Once he knew I had it, he had to make sure I got some use from it. Keeping me on the line, he had me fill it with tepid water, then fill myself, only two bulbs' worth to start, fourteen ounces. He instructed me to insert my butt plug and proceeded to chat away with me on the phone.

It was embarrassing and uncomfortable, but the feeling of being full was very erotic to me, and I will admit the humiliation factor wasn't hurting matters too much. Jeff chatted about benign things while I squirmed on the bed, worried that I was going to leak my water and make a mess. I could hear the amusement in his voice when he'd ask me a question, and it would take all my control to be able to answer. I was in subspace, feeling fragile and vulnerable, trying desperately to carry on my end of the conversation regardless of the distraction I was experiencing. I'd had the forethought to bring a towel with me and hoped it would be enough if I had an accident. I was glad he was not in the room with me, but at the same time I wished that he were. Comfort me, please. I'm way out of my element here.

After about ten minutes, he asked me how I was feeling and had me describe the physical and emotional trauma I was experiencing for him. I had cramping, pressure, a feeling of being out of control of my body. I was fighting to hold everything in. I begged him to let me release it. I was laughing at my predicament but at the same time I was on the edge of panic. He was enjoying this way too much I thought.

Finally Jeff allowed me to leave the phone to relieve myself. What a relief when I expelled the water. I came back to the phone and he praised me for doing this incredibly personal act for him. He crooned to me, whispering his encouragement in my ear, guiding me to touch myself, to bring myself to climax for him. I was putty in his hands.

I thought about our experiment for a few days, trying to decide how I felt about it. The humiliation made me hot, but I wasn't sure about the physical sensations of the enema. I had so much social programming regarding this issue. It was dirty and private and dark and personal. But I know I pleased him by doing his bidding, and that, in the end, was my goal.

For a couple of weeks, we worked on my tolerance for the idea of enemas and the feelings that came with them, continuing to experiment on the phone so I could get used to the feelings alone and learn to accept them. I was just beginning to get comfortable with the whole idea when Jeff called me with a new set of instructions. I was to fill myself with two bulbs of water and expel them after ten minutes. Then I was to repeat the exercise again in two hours. Then, at 6:00 P.M., I was to fill myself with three bulbs of water, insert my butt plug, and wait for him. Wait for him? Oh no, could I do this? I spent the rest of the week worrying about it.

The day arrived. I took care of my regular routine, showering, shaving, perfuming, getting myself all fluffed and pretty for Jeff. Then I began his special instructions. Two bulbs of water were easy for me by this time, and I did as I was told without a hitch. Filling myself with three bulbs was worrisome—it was the most water I had ever held—but I expected I would be able to manage it and tried not to worry about it too much.

He was late, that night. I was sitting at the top of the stairs waiting for him to come, wiggling and squirming to try to retain the water and ease the mild cramping I was feeling. It was the tremendous pressure building inside me that set the panic off. I went into the bathroom so that if I couldn't manage to maintain control at least I'd be near the toilet. He called to tell me he was on his way. I begged him to allow me to release my water. I was almost in tears as I told him where I was sitting and how bad the pressure was. He allowed me to relieve myself.

Over the next couple of weeks, he had me fill myself with three bulbs of water and then wait for him to arrive at the house. The first time, I was permitted to expel as soon as he arrived. The next time, I had to sit at his feet for a while as he watched my discomfort and embarrassment before I was allowed to relieve myself. He enjoyed seeing me fight for control of my body. He enjoyed the fact that I did not beg or ask for relief but bore my discomfort until he granted me permission to use the washroom. He never came with me. He let me go on my own and watched me as I awkwardly dashed down the hall to my salvation.

I found, over time, that I wanted more than what I was getting from this experience. I wanted him to be the one to fill me. I wanted to be completely humiliated in front of him. I wanted to be at his mercy, his control. I wanted to be his entertainment. I wish I had remembered the saying "Be careful what you wish for."

Jeff came to the house on a Saturday afternoon. I was dressed in a black miniskirt, black stockings, black garters, black heels, and a black-and-white tank top. He loves miniskirts and was quite pleased with me. We chatted for a bit, then he wanted to poke around on my computer. He sat at the desk and I sat on the floor beside him. It was then he sent me off for my toys.

I retrieved my toy box and set it on the floor beside him. He reached in and took out my tweezer clamps and told me to remove my top. I did, and he attached the clamps to my tiny pink nipples, tightly, painfully. He then had me turn my back to him. He lifted my skirt and began to inspect my ass, slipping a finger into my moist pussy, pulling on my labia, poking and prodding my sex. Then he said, "Go fill your bulb, slave." My heart skipped a beat. What I had been hoping for was about to happen.

I returned with the bulb full of very warm water and handed it to him. He had me turn around again and bend over. I was standing about three feet from him, bent over at the waist, my hands gripping my ankles. I felt his hands on my ass and the nozzle of the bulb being inserted. My heart raced as I felt the water flow into me. I was a little embarrassed, but not too much. I was actually quite pleased that he thought I was ready to expose myself to him in this fashion. He handed me the bulb and sent me back twice for more, which had me at about twenty-one ounces of fluid. That was my comfort level. But my comfort level was about to be surpassed.

I was in front of him, bent over, ass exposed, freshly injected with the third bulb. I heard him rummage in the toy box, and then I felt him take hold of my pussy lips. I felt spots of pain between my legs as he attached my alligator clamps, one to each lip. They hurt like the clamps on my nipples. I heard the buzz of a vibrator and felt the light touch of the tip as it traced around my pussy. It felt nice and I held my position as he toyed with me.

The real trouble started when he sent me for a fourth bulb of water. I tried to keep my legs apart as I walked to the bathroom, but he told me to walk properly. My pussy hurt as my thighs brushed the chain hanging from the clamps; I felt full and awkward. I returned and handed him the bulb. Again he filled me. Twenty-eight ounces now, and I could really feel the fullness. He had me stay put, bent over with my ass and muff displayed for him. After a few minutes he took the vibrator to me again. Teasing and tickling my clit, arousing me to the point that I was straining to bring my backside nearer to him. He told me to get another bulb.

Terror rose in my heart. I knew I was over my limit. I had never held four bulbs of liquid inside me before, and certainly not five. Walking was becoming very difficult, especially since Jeff didn't want to see any hint of the discomfort I was in. My gait was ridiculously awkward, given the water he had flushed inside me, my heels, and the clamps. I tried to be ladylike as I walked down the hall but I'm sure I looked as if I had just got off a three-day camel ride.

I looked at the dreaded bathroom tap and with a huge sigh of resignation, turned the water on for the fifth time, and

adjusted the temperature. Carefully I filled the bulb and wad-
dled back to where Jeff sat, watching me, so evilly entertained
by my discomfort. I handed the bulb to him again and waited
for my instructions. He directed me back to the same position,
bent over, ass exposed. Only this time I was trembling. I can't
tell you whether it was fear or anticipation but I was so completely out of control. I was far beyond the limits I had been
secure with only weeks ago. I felt the nozzle enter my anus.

He talked to me as he squeezed the last bulb inside me.
He was being so kind and gentle and loving, telling me how
happy he was I accepted his liquid. How proud I made him
by trusting him this much. His voice was velvet in my ears;
smooth, calm, and soft. How could I ever refuse him anything?
I whimpered as he removed the nozzle, terrified I'd spring a
leak and make a mess. I focused on his voice, hypnotized by
the rhythm in his tone. My body trembled.

I stayed bent over, and he caressed my ass, moving his
hands in circles as he worked to ease my fear. His hands slid
down between my thighs, and he finally removed the clamps
on my pussy. I cried out as he released each one and gasped
as he quickly thrust two fingers deep inside me. I was flooded
with fear and pleasure and pain. My mind was spinning as
each emotion and sensation bombarded me. I was shaking
uncontrollably when he removed his fingers and told me to
stand. Confused, fearful, I was desperate for him to take care
of me. Unable to think or act on my own behalf, I was completely at his mercy, mentally and physically.

I turned to face him, and he slid his fingers into my mouth,
one at a time, so that I could clean each one. He liked me to
taste my own dew, and he liked to kiss it from my lips, which
was exactly his next move.

The warmth of his lips made me want to melt, and I had to hang on to him to keep upright. Our tongues danced together, his teeth occasionally biting down on my tongue binding my face to his. This made me giggle, which would pull on my tongue, so he'd bite down harder.

He liked to tease me like this. How many times had he deliberately put me in a spot where there was nothing for me to do but accept the pain he liked to sneak to me? It was to keep my attention, he would say, when I accused him of sabotaging me. And here I thought he always had my attention.

My tongue still between his teeth, he reached down to the clamps on my nipples and removed each one. I was close to tears as the pain burned bright on my tender flesh. He released my tongue and held me tight, lightly massaging the blood back to my nipples. I held my breath and buried my head in his shoulder until the pain subsided enough to be able to look up into his deep brown eyes.

His smile lit up his face, his eyes twinkled; he whispered that soon I'd be able to release my burden. With that, he reached behind him and brought out a blindfold. I dropped my hands to my sides and turned away to make it easier for him to tie it. Slowly and deliberately, he turned me around a couple times so that I lost my orientation to the room. I was now in his full control. He took my hand and led me away.

I didn't know where he was leading me. I was so confused by the physical stimulation of the evening that I couldn't maintain a concrete idea of where I was in my own home. Carefully, so as not to trip in my heels, I allowed myself to be led. It was only when I was turned and felt the linoleum under my feet that I knew where he was taking me.

Jeff backed me up to the toilet and helped me sit. My heart

pounded in my ears as I realized it was really about to happen. He was going to make me expel all the water he'd been injecting into my rectum. I was mortified and excited all at the same time. I could feel my cunt lubricate as my juices flowed freely. I waited for the command to release.

The command didn't come. Instead, I heard his zipper.

I wondered what he was going to do next. I needed to release the water so badly. I wasn't sure how much longer I could stand the weight and the pressure. Sitting on the open toilet only made the desire stronger, and I strained to hold it for him.

I was having difficulty with the whole scenario. Everything I had been taught my entire life told me this was bad. I shouldn't be in this position, in a bathroom with a man standing in front of me. Had I no shame? No, I had none. I was his slut and his slave, here for his pleasure, and if he wanted me this humble I was going to live through it, even if I felt like dying inside. I felt the head of his cock press against my lips, and I opened to accept him.

"Hold on, little one, your time is near." With that, he began to gently fuck my face.

Jeff was much more gentle with me that day than he had been in the past. He eased himself into me, giving me time to tongue and lubricate him. I sucked him into my mouth, wanting him to fill me more than ever before. I wanted my mouth to be as full of him as my ass was of water. I took him deeply, urgently. He praised me as I sucked. He allowed me to control the speed at which his long, hard cock slid in and out of my mouth.

The more I worked my mouth on him, the faster he began to pump. I was desperate to release myself, but I held my focus to his cock. He continued to praise me and continued to pump inside of me. He gripped my hair and was pulling my head toward him as he thrust his hips forward. I was aroused. I was far more than aroused, my clit was swollen and I imagined how glossy it must look covered in my pussy juice. I needed to release my water and I needed him to grip my clit and I needed him to fuck my face. I needed everything, I wanted everything. I sucked harder and deeper, trying to show him the passion raging inside me.

I felt his cock stiffen, and I knew he was about to come. I wanted his wad to be forced down my throat. I gasped for air between thrusts, my hands gripping the cheeks of his ass, holding on to him to keep upright, to brace myself for what was about to come to me.

"Release yourself, slave." His voice was ragged as he began his own release into the back of my throat.

My excitement peaked the moment I felt his heated seed shooting down my throat, the moment my muscles could finally let go of the weight of the water pressing against my insides. The water gushed from me. I had never felt greater humiliation. It was far worse than when he pushed the water into me. I closed my eyes behind the blindfold.

Shame and euphoria battled in my mind. I knew I had done my job, I knew I had pleased him. But even in that moment of joy was the shame of what was expelling from my body, the relief from the pressure, the embarrassment of what was happening to me physically, my complete loss of physical control, the new sensation of the water flushing out my most private place. Was I happy? Was I embarrassed? I couldn't name what I was feeling.

He continued to hold my hair tightly, pulling my face into

his pubic hair, making my breathing near-impossible, and the water continued to flow from my ass. The intense confusion, the sexual tension, the knowledge that I pleased him finally took over my body. I was surprised by my own orgasm. I moaned. My arms wrapped around his hips. I couldn't control the flow of water, I couldn't control the spasms of pleasure, I couldn't control my need for air. For a brief moment, my body was completely out of my conscious control—all it could do was react to sensation and emotion.

He let go of my hair, and his hands slid to my face, gently pulling my head away. I was gasping for air, my body was shaking, and I was still blindfolded. He guided me to my feet and held me close, kissing me deeply, this time without biting my tongue, but prodding it to taste his own essence. I felt him take a towel to my bottom and he softly patted the wetness from my ass cheeks. One last act of power for him and humiliation for me.

Without a word, Jeff led me out of the bathroom and into my bedroom. He took me to the bed, laid me down, and wrapped me in my big feather quilt. He climbed in beside me and finally removed my blindfold. He'd kept the lights very dim, and when the blindfold came off I was looking into his deep, chocolate-brown eyes. He smiled at me and kissed my forehead.

"You were a very good girl today, my pet. Rest, now."

He held me in his arms and I closed my eyes again, this time to sleep.

BECKY

Kay Jaybee

Regardless of my warnings, she had applied
for the administrative assistant vacancy at the
office where I work. Perhaps I was wrong to
be wary. Becky had always listened eagerly
to the tales I told before dismissively saying,
"Don't be ridiculous, that sort of thing doesn't
really happen," quickly followed by, "so what
happened next?" Maybe I shouldn't have told
her anything. It's too late now.

Becky's face looked as if it would remain
in a state of shock forever. Her gray skirt
was hunched around her slim waist and her
thong lay in tatters after its surgical removal
with the boss's scissors. She stood stock still
as the correction stool was placed reverently
in its familiar position in the very center of
the office.

She kept repeating over and over again, "It was an accident, an accident. I never meant to spill the coffee. An accident." I felt for her, she blinking in disbelief as her fellow workers followed their boss's instructions and came to stand around her and the stool.

"Bend." It wasn't a request. Our aging but terrifyingly fit boss was ordering her without even raising his voice. I willed her to do as she was told, for her own sake.

"Bend now." Becky could feel the danger of refusal in the air; we all could. It was almost tangible. Our colleagues were barely breathing as they focused on the stool. Most were thankful that it wasn't them; some had been so broken by submission that they wished it were.

Unsure of exactly how to position herself, Becky clumsily lowered her waist over the wide wooden seat, holding herself steady by grabbing the legs with her outstretched arms. With his usual economy of movement the boss shifted her further onto the stool so that her ass was deliciously exposed, while her legs balanced precariously on her high heels. Then he fastened her taut limbs in place with thick black bootlaces, carefully designed to cut into the sinner's skin should she wriggle too much.

Then he paused, turning his back on the young woman, who was still battling to comprehend how accidentally slopping a mug of coffee could result in such chastisement. The boss went to the closet in the corner of the room. When he returned, he was holding a long, thin, white cane.

Becky's eyes never left the cane. Her face had taken on the pallor of a ghost as the final shred of hope that this was all some sick initiation ceremony dissolved. What the hell would have happened if she'd spilled the whole cup of coffee?

The sound of the first crack across her tight pale buttocks was drowned out by her shocked scream. Yes, it really is happening. I warned you.

The second, then the third, left smart red lines as the cane connected with her prone ass. Becky's screams were reaching epic proportions and the boss was obviously getting bored of the noise. Stopping to undo his tie, he wrapped it into a makeshift gag and swiftly tied it around Becky's flushed face.

The forth lash, the fifth. Becky was biting for all she was worth into the thin strip of material. The humiliation of her situation would surely be going around and around her confused mind, as the silent workforce watched her enforced submission. By the sixth stroke she was hardly making a sound, her concentration on simply surviving the ordeal. On the eighth stroke it happened. We all heard it.

She whimpered. Her reaction was changing; she was reaching the crossover point between unwanted pain and desired pain. Perhaps I'd been wrong about Becky. Perhaps this wasn't her first submission. How well did I know her after all? No one here had ever responded that way the first time before. She had seemed genuinely shocked and frightened by the situation, but suddenly I began to suspect she had her own motives for being here.

Her buttocks, now scarlet, bruised, and striped, gave off a throbbing heat as the boss hesitated. He'd heard the subtle alteration in her voice; he waited just long enough for a tiny sigh to escape her moist lips before bringing the cane down with precision onto the exact spot where the previous stroke had hit.

Then it stopped. She was left there shaking and unfulfilled, as the whip was lovingly returned to its home. All the workers returned to their desks, once again mindful of the consequences of making a mistake.

This was the worst stage. During my first humiliation, I had been sure the lashing itself would be the worst thing that could happen. I hadn't counted on the shame factor. Surely Becky would be feeling it now as the air-conditioning wafted across her stinging flesh. Would she be grappling with her thoughts? "How had this happened?" "Why don't they let me go now?" "How will I ever look anyone in the eye again?" Maybe she hadn't yet noticed that the people here do not look each other in the eye. In this office the safest option is definitely the meek one.

The blood would have rushed to her head by now. She'd be wondering if there was more to come. I had warned her, and she hadn't believed me. Or had she? I looked furtively across my desk as she remained motionless, either too scared or too sensible to speak. Even if she was stupid enough to ask how long she would remain there, we couldn't have told her. It depended on how long the boss and his assistant took in their separate office.

I saw them once. The boss had rightly sensed I was beginning to enjoy my punishments, and had decided a further level of correction was required. My ass burning from a thorough paddling, I had to watch, helpless, bound to the desk, as the boss received relief from the arousal my disciplining had obviously caused him.

I have never heard his assistant speak. She is simply referred to as Miss Harriet, but I have no idea if Harriet is her first or last name. I do know that she loves her work, and I suspect she fears that he will grow weary of her one day. Perhaps that's why she never speaks—to keep an air of mystery. All this went through my head as I lay there naked, my weighty tits crushed against the writing surface, my aching legs dangling over the edge, not quite reaching the floor, and my ass smarting as I was kept somewhere between agony and ecstasy.

He hadn't said anything to Miss Harriet. Just a look at his face seemed to tell her exactly what to do. First she stepped neatly out of her immaculate A-line skirt, then she slipped off her crisp white blouse. I tried to resist drawing breath as her beautiful bodice and stockings revealed her pantiless, heart-shaped pussy. Not that this was on view for long, as she bent, without prompting, across the arm of the large black leather armchair in the corner of the room and waited.

I couldn't take my eyes off her. She had placed herself in a position of humiliation with every shred of dignity intact. Her buttocks, however, told their own story. The dark-pink welts that neatly crisscrossed her regularly bronzed flesh looked angry. They obviously rarely had time to heal between assaults.

Her master had already taken off his clothes, revealing a well-toned figure for a man of his years, his hard dick showing just how much he had enjoyed my correction. The new paddle he selected for his work had four hard rubber studs encased in a smooth black cover. I was just imagining the agony it might inflict when I saw for myself. Although my view was partially obstructed by the boss, I strained against my bonds so I could see this fascinating creature take punishment simply because she was there and his hard-on had to be dealt with. My boss's skill with the chosen weapon was evident. One, two, three, the paddle came down with speed. I could see indents appear in her flesh as the nodules cut in. Yet, despite her already damaged skin, she shed not a drop of blood.

All that time, Miss Harriet had made no sound. Her concentration must have been incredible as the vicious strokes lashed her rose buttocks. I counted each stroke as I felt my own helpless, wasted, liquid ooze down my thighs onto the desk's conveniently placed blotting paper. The assistant's steady breathing had become shallow and urgent by the tenth lash, and the boss's own had turned into an animal grunt as suddenly, on the twelfth, he dropped his weapon, grabbed her hips, and pulled her toward him, thrusting his painfully hard cock into her waiting ass. Her cry was more one of relief than of pain as he hammered into her.

I lay there, desperate for attention, imagining what it would be like to hold the whip hand for a change; to be able to counteract my corrective measures by touching her soft skin, licking her engorged nipples, kissing her panting lips.

Then it was over. He growled his release as she rubbed herself against the chair to bring herself off. Miss Harriet, silent once more, turned and passed him a handkerchief to clean himself up before dismissing herself with an incline of her delicate head. I was left there for another hour. No one touched me. It was a worse agony than the lashes.

Becky stayed. I wasn't sure she would turn up the following day; many before her hadn't. However, as she sat at her desk her eyes weren't cast down like her peers'; they had a defiant glint to them that I feared could be dangerous. It wasn't that much of a surprise to me when, two days later, Becky dropped a pile of recently sorted filing on the floor directly in front of the boss's door. "Nerves," one of my colleagues whispered. I wasn't so sure. I couldn't help wondering if she had done it deliberately, to see what might happen next.

Just as before, the stool was positioned in the center of the circle. This time, however, Becky positioned herself, with no word of prompting, on the hard surface. She revealed her own, still slightly bruised, rump and offered up her wrists to be bound.

The boss watched her with interest and shook his head. You never got what you wanted here. Becky was left, standing there, ass exposed, as he put the stool away again. Waiting. No one got the upper hand in this office.

He opened the closet and, without a word, beckoned her to approach. I held my breath, already turned on by the prospect of what was to come. To my eternal shame, it is why I stay here. This place had changed my tastes. There was no going back. I watched.

It was an unusual closet. From floor to ceiling in height, it had an increased depth hidden behind its gray metal doors. The shelves along the walls were set well back, so that at least two people could occupy the remaining space with the doors closed. On every shelf there was a collection of instruments: canes, whips, paddles, nipple clamps. There was all the necessary material to keep a correction freak going for years: ribbons, ropes, cuffs, chains, gags. The more you looked, the more your heart froze and your eyes widened. Becky looked. Her face revealed nothing.

Miss Harriet had silently come out of her office. Without a word she stood behind Becky and helped her off with her remaining clothes. Becky was so beautiful. I realized I hadn't really looked at her properly before. I already wanted to touch; I began to imagine her beating my breasts with a short stick and then soothing them with her tongue.

I came back to reality. Such feelings must not be displayed

here. Becky was now just inside the closet doors, facing her audience. She seemed to shine. How had she got to this point so quickly? It had taken me many beatings before I had learned to enjoy it, and even after nearly eighteen months I could never be so open about it. I still have the shame. Maybe I need it.

Becky stared through us as she looked straight ahead. Miss Harriet had taken one of her slim wrists and was tying it to a conveniently placed hook on one of the shelves with a silk cord. Then she secured the other wrist, then the ankles, and finally she snapped a thin silver collar securely around Becky's neck, its long leather cord dangling provocatively between her breasts.

Miss Harriet stepped out of the closet and looked to her boss for approval. He nodded. I could clearly see, when I dared to glance, that his dick was straining against his suit trousers. They shut the doors of the closet, and we all heard Becky gasp. She had expected pain, arousal. They had given her nothing.

No one could concentrate. Returning to our work was impossibly hard.

An hour after the doors had been closed, our boss came out of his office, his slightly creased clothes revealing that Miss Harriet's services had been called upon once again. As he walked between our desks, the tension was intense. He wanted to punish someone. Any excuse would do.

He signaled to Miss Harriet, who brought the stool forward. "Congratulations," he said. "Despite events," (he gestured to the closet) "you have all managed some work. Not much. But something." He paced around the stool, like a panther waiting to pounce. "Like me, I suspect you have all been rather turned on by recent events. Some of you" (he looked straight at me) "will be literally wetting your underpants with anticipation. Just waiting for the crop to strike. Others are still torn between running and staying." He paused and surveyed his workforce. "But you will all stay. Every day I wonder who will fail to turn up for work, but each day you all come."

No one dared to speak. I could feel my breath scratching my throat as he continued. "It is not in my nature to give rewards, but in this case I think it would provide an apt lesson for our newest recruit." He again gestured to the closet. "Becky cannot hear us through those doors, although she can see around her. The light inside is sufficient for her to be able to examine at close quarters all the instruments that she so unwisely volunteered herself to experience."

"For one hour only she will be your slave. I will open the doors and she will be yours to do with as you like. Do not waste this experience. It is very unlikely to ever happen again."

My eyes must have lit up, because he bestowed upon me one of his rare and rather unnerving smiles. "Yes, I thought you'd like that. But I am also sure that you would benefit from your own ass being warmed. I know I would enjoy performing the task for you."

I glanced at the stool. Was I that obvious? I wasn't like Becky. I could never have engineered a situation like this, but he was right, and I could feel my nipples harden at the thought of the tingling pain that would spread across my buttocks to my already damp pussy.

"Strip." He ordered, and I obeyed. My hands shook slightly as I fumbled with my blouse buttons, and the slightly bent clasp of my bra. Finally naked, I cast my eyes down. Yes, I needed the shame. The wood felt cold beneath my skin as I offered up my ass, hands unbound, holding on to the stool's sturdy legs. I could see the closet doors, now open, as I watched between my legs, my head hanging down. Becky's legs were still bound, quivering slightly. Being shut in the closet for so long had obviously taken away some of her bravado. Doubt had had time to creep in, just as our boss had intended it to.

He was in the closet. Was he selecting a weapon for me or for her? Would I be gagged this time? It appeared that I was to be trusted to be still, and would not be bound.

"Becky." The boss was clearly speaking to her, but addressing the whole office at the same time. "As you can see, you are not the only one who has chosen to feel the sting today." He was standing behind me. There was something in his hand, but I couldn't see what it was. How much pain? Was it a cane or a whip? My question was answered by the crack of a leather strap as it made contact with my tensed skin. Despite my determination not to, I automatically flinched and a shocked cry came from my lips, instantly resulting in a harder slap, then another, faster and faster.

I couldn't keep still. Without the usual bonds, the desire to wriggle after each lash was incredibly strong, and by the fifth hit I could feel two pairs of cold masculine hands on my inflamed flesh, holding me firmly in place. The result of their touch was almost enough to tip me over the edge.

Becky was beginning to whine. I opened my eyes and saw that she was receiving some attention of her own. I could just hear a faint smack over the crack of my own punishment. My head was full of pictures of Becky's torment, which must have been doubled by the act of watching mine. I wanted her very badly.

BECKY

It ended as quickly as it had begun. The extreme burn
which had spread across my ass was tingling as my brain
slowly registered that the pain had stopped. The hands which
had been pressing into me slipped under my arms and pulled
me upright. My head spun as my stiff body became accustomed to standing, and for a moment I rested heavily on my
captor's arms.

They brought me before Becky, and I watched as the boss
took over from Miss Harriet, who had clearly been driving
Becky to distraction by alternatively slapping her distended
tits and rubbing her nipples with a silk handkerchief. The
tears which had been silently pouring from Becky's face had
dried, and she collected herself for whatever was to follow. I
wanted to remind her that she started this, but all I could do
was look at her.

The boss took one long, hard swipe at her engorged nipples
with the belt he had so recently used on me. I couldn't decide
if the scream that left Becky's lips was one of relief, sheer
frustration, or pain.

He released her feet and wrists before taking the leather
cord which hung across her chest and pulling her out of the
closet. He gave the cord to me and said to us, "She's all yours.
One hour only." He left then, grabbing a couple of chains
before pushing Miss Harriet rather too roughly toward his
office door.

I didn't move. Becky and I were still naked, but no one else
was. The silence lasted for about thirty seconds until the spell
was broken and the men who had been holding me down
snapped to attention. Both ran to the open closet and grabbed
what they wanted. Before I could think, the biting claws of
a pair of cruel silver nipple clamps were making Becky cry

out in agony as her tortured breasts flushed in response. Her arms were held while the others watched, fascinated, as canes, whips, and paddles were grabbed from their hooks. Becky's eyes were wide. She began to suffer an assault that was evidently the result of months of pent-up frustration from my fellow workers. Her breasts, arms, thighs, and buttocks all took a simultaneous lashing as she stood there. She screamed and yelled, but her eyes clearly shouted *Don't stop!* and she relished every stroke. Sticky liquid was seeping out of her wet snatch as I watched, transfixed by this amazing creature. She looked at me beseechingly and I could not deny her. I let go of the cord, pushed past one of my colleagues who was pinching the underside of her swollen breasts, and kissed her. I had never kissed anyone like that. It was as if I was saving her, taking her beyond the agony of her deliciously pain-racked body. Her anguish was silenced by my hungry lips, and I moaned into her as the lashes began to crack across me as well.

An hour later, I gently removed the clamps, kissing the damaged nipples to make them better, and slipped her crumpled blouse back over her warmed chest.

Then we all returned to our desks to work.

There was never any question that I would go home with her. How I didn't come as we simply held hands on the walk to her flat I shall never know.

No sooner had we got through the door than our clothes were in a heap and Becky pulled me into her bedroom. She laid me down on her soft coffee-colored duvet and pulled a large battered suitcase from the corner of the room. It was full of every type of sex toy I had ever seen. Even our boss would have been envious of such a collection.

As I allowed myself to be gagged and bound by this pale beauty, I finally understood why I had been unable to talk her out of applying for the job. This was what she had desired from the very beginning, and for that I will be eternally grateful.

ELECTRIC RAZOR

Irma Wimple

She discovered it while shaving her legs.

She paused, letting the electric razor rest against her thigh. The sensations that traveled to her delicates from the vibrating razor captivated her. She stopped shaving and moved the butt end of the razor higher and higher, until the resonating device was nestled against her womanhood, pressed close and high, as she closed her legs tightly. Her head tipped back and she lost herself in the sensations.

Slowly the iris of her awareness shrank down to the warmth beating between her legs. The sounds of the stereo, the draining bath, the traffic, the feeling of the cold ceramic tile under her feet, the rush of air from the furnace all faded. She knew only the interaction of the razor's buzz and her own heartbeat, which she could feel more strongly now in her clitoris than in her chest. She held still for a long time, holding the razor against herself. She felt the need to move, and made tiny pelvic thrusts, holding the razor still. The tiniest movements felt so good to her, and escalated her incrementally each time—finally, to a place she had only known in dreams.

With no warning she crested the hill, fell over the edge, and strong throbbing contractions bloomed from deep under her clitoris, threatening her focus on the hand holding the razor. In ever-spreading ripples, the intense orgasm throbbed countless beats, sending warm pleasure daggers into her entire body. It was almost too much to bear.

She was silent and still—anyone watching her would only see her catch and hold her breath. No one would witness the red heat pulsing within her before it subsided, and she took a deep quavering breath, and a dreamy beatific smile was left upon her face.

She left the razor where it was and soon climaxed two more times; smaller throbbing aftershocks that threatened to overload her pleasure centers. Afterward, she stumbled to the living room in her terry-cloth robe, curled up in a beanbag chair, and fell profoundly asleep in a sunbeam.

She found other things in her flat which produced similar effects when used unconventionally. Her tiny food processor, pureeing spinach or beans, could release her with a quick shotgun orgasm after a day of speed and tension. She had to practice pressing against it in exactly the right position; reaching her orgasm required navigating a narrow channel of sensation. If she deviated too much, she was swept around it in an eddy and it passed her by, leaving her sweaty, itchy, and frustrated. Placing the processor on a kitchen chair and standing against it, knees bent, worked remarkably once she had awkwardly discovered it.

She began to eat a lot of processed food and soups.

Sitting on the vacuum cleaner took a long time, but the orgasms came from deep within her and lasted and lasted, until she had to fall, squirming and sighing, off her perch on the base of the machine. She humped the floor then, or her John Lennon pillow, until the tiny clutching aftershocks came and came, erasing her identity, collapsed and carpet-burned until morning.

She acquired the habit of hanging around the laundry room and sitting on the washer pretending to read a book during the spin cycle. The other tenement denizens suspected nothing—only watching her eyes becoming fixed on the text, and the clutching and holding of her breath would give away her booming squeezing laundry-room climaxes. She would sit, her undies feeling tighter and tighter, a swelling thumping rising from below until she thought she would pee her pants. Then the silent invisible wave would squeeze and squeeze her hot throbbing sex until she nearly fell over.

She had an old drill which was slightly off-center, and when she turned it outward and held the butt of the drill against her mound, she rapidly climbed through the sensations to a short, flutteringly rapid and intense orgasm. She could repeat these by reapplying the machine as soon as she could again control her hand, until she was exhausted and felt her entire abdominal area cramp as it would during her period. She would not be horny for days after one of these, but a bit sore and bruised.

She began to shop at home-and-kitchen-supply stores during off-hours, so she could turn on the appliances and feel their motors. She acquired an ability to predict the type of orgasm from the feel of the machine in the store. She bought a breadmaker, whose kneading paddles set her throbbing but left her unsatisfied, and she had to go use the electric razor to bring herself off. The razor always gave her the longest, most satisfying, and most multiple climaxes. She turned back to it when the other machines didn't have the depth, the focus that the tiny rechargeable razor gave her.

She bought a cordless electric screwdriver that she would hold between her legs with no head attached while she was sitting at the computer. An hour would go by and she would forget it was there, as its charge started running out, and suddenly she would need to get off the chair, clasp something soft between her legs, and squeeze and squeeze until a tiny, soft, clutching orgasm reached up to her from the depths. The magnitude of these was low, but the duration was high, and they left her smiling and sleepy.

Summer came, and she found that she could lean against the frame of her boxy window fan, pressing the rounded corner into her pubic mound through her clothes. She pushed against the vibrating fan, very carefully, getting the vibrations in exactly the right place. The climax would come without warning, again, lofting her over the unseen barrier, and she slid, throbbing, down, down, down into hot red squeezing pulsing oblivion.

She rarely made any outward show of passion during these machine-driven orgasms. The entire torrent, the pulsing flood of sensation, was so internal and private that little escaped to the outside world. She did not need to moan and fling herself about. The quieter she was, the more intensely she felt the sensations. Her eyes were always closed to keep her focus narrow, within her, avoiding distractions and stimuli from outside.

This new world of oblivion in climax fascinated her, and she wanted to explore all corners and depths of feeling she could attain. She had only slept with one man, her inept and distant high school boyfriend, and never once achieved anything near her electric razor orgasm. She owned dozens of electric, cordless, and windup machines, and became very skilled at creating a climax to suit her mood.

But she was lonely.

One day she went down to the laundry room to empty the dryer. There was a man there, lanky black hair still wet from a shower, unshaven, in a tight V-neck white T-shirt and jeans, barefoot. He was reading a book, sitting on her favorite washer, on spin cycle.

She smiled.

JUST WORDS

Donna George Storey

I told him words wouldn't do it.

Not X-rated e-mails.

Or sizzling phone sex.

Or "You know how much I love you, babe."

And certainly not "I'm sorry I have to give up three weeks of great sex with you to go to Europe to kiss client ass for my fat boss who will pocket all the profit and maybe if I'm lucky give me a measly bonus at the end of the fiscal year"—although a little honesty about what's really going on here with his new job would be a step in the right direction.

What I needed was flesh. Heat. The music of his moans in my ear. His sturdy hands stroking my breasts. His finger teasing my asshole. His cock buried so deep inside my red, grasping mouth of a cunt, I didn't feel hungry anymore.

He couldn't take me there with just words.

To his credit, he did deliver the goods the evening before he left for London. It was just like the early days, when we spent whole weekends tangled together in the sheets, staggering out of bed only to get another bottle of wine or pay the pizza delivery guy. He made me come five times, twice riding his cock, twice on his tongue and once as he pinched my nipples and spanked my ass while I "secretly" rubbed my pussy against the mattress. I treated him to a postprandial crème de menthe blow job, along with my usual repertory of tricks to tease his tender parts. I liked the way he groaned and called out my name, but I really hoped our fuckfest would make him say other words.

Such as: "Fuck *them,* I'm staying with you."

Instead, he stumbled off to the airport, with a bleary-eyed wink and a promise he'd e-mail every morning and night, and we'd have a nice long phone call—on the company's dollar—every Saturday afternoon.

Still floating in the afterglow, I convinced myself that it was enough, that we could make it through three weeks apart with just words.

Until I got his first e-mail.

He wrote that he was really looking forward to our "date" on Saturday, but in the meantime he wanted me to refrain from any self-pleasuring activity—he actually used that lady-librarian expression—for the rest of the week. To make it all the hotter when he finally brought me off over the phone.

Yeah, right.

I gave a nasty little laugh, pulled my nightgown up to my waist, and jilled off right in front of the computer. Now and then I'd take a break and type a few more sentences of my reply.

Hey, lover boy. I think it's time for a little confession. When you're gone I keep myself plenty satisfied with the help of two tireless lovers. At night they take turns: One strokes my nipples into hard little points, while the other goes down to do the slip-slide in my wet pussy. Every morning, I wake up with a tight ache between my legs—don't kid yourself, girls don't rise at dawn, it's just hidden away inside. So me and my fuck buddies do it then, too, and I'm feeling so sexy from my morning quickie I put on a short skirt and boots, or the jeans that push right up in my crotch to go to work at the bookstore. You'd never let me out of the apartment dressed that way, but you aren't here to stop me, are you? I get so itchy I can't help but shake my butt when I guide the gray-haired married men over to the finance section. And I always make sure the cute young guys need a book from the lowest shelf, so I can bend over and give them an eyeful of ass or cleavage, depending on the angle. Yesterday, I snuck off to the alcove by the poetry journals, where I let lover number one climb under my skirt, while number two yanked my sweater over my tits and tweaked and pinched them until I came so hard my head practically blew off. Moments after I straightened my clothes, a really hot guy—one of those ponytailed literary types—walked in and gave me a long, knowing look. I'm sure he knew what I'd been doing. He could probably smell me, too. The idea got me so turned on I had another encounter in the ladies' room. But maybe next time

I'll just fuck the guy against the bookshelf. The truth is, I'm having such a wild time I don't miss you at all. Why would I give up all this fun for an hour of yakety-yak phone sex with you?

Think again, buddy.

I clicked the Send icon, spread my legs wider around the chair, and climaxed right then and there on my dancing finger. Loudly.

Sure, maybe I was taunting him, but it served him right. Besides, a lot of what I wrote was true. I did get turned on when I was working at the bookstore. I wouldn't admit it to him, but it wasn't so much the customers as the words that excited me, especially when they were packaged between the covers of a new book. I loved to stroke its crisp pages, then spread it open wide and bend to breathe in the perfume of fresh paper and ink. I rarely started reading it at the beginning—I wanted to take a book by surprise, slip right inside its soft middle. The good ones always got under my skin to lift me, transport me, to another time, another place, another body. A steamy sex scene would always send me straight to the staff ladies' room for relief.

And when he was away, I usually did soothe myself to sleep with some action between my legs, then woke up horny and took the necessary steps to quench that fire, too. But busy as they were, my hands never quite stilled the longing deep in my belly the way he could do with his fingers, tongue, and cock.

And so, I had to admit, the last part of the e-mail was a bald-faced lie. I did miss him. Bad.

When I saw his reply in my in-box the next morning, I felt a twinge of worry that I'd gone too far with the insatiable-slut revenge fantasy. But he didn't seem mad. In fact he apologized and agreed he had no right to put limits on my private activities, especially since he couldn't help jacking off after he read the part about me playing with myself in the poetry annex. While he stroked his cock, he imagined he'd been the one to catch me with my hand up my skirt and pictured all the ways he'd "punish" me for it.

But, he suggested again with all due respect, for my own enjoyment I might consider abstaining on Friday night and Saturday morning. He'd come up with some new ideas for our date, and he was pretty sure I'd agree they were worth waiting for. He promised to send instructions on how to prepare myself by Saturday morning.

I had to laugh again. While he'd certainly picked up on my intention to make him jealous with the public masturbation scene, he was apparently slow to grasp my broader message of female autonomy.

Still, I had to admit the word *instructions* made me tingle a little *down there*. I even took a little vacation from tickling the clam as the weekend drew near.

Of course, I got up extra early to check my e-mail Saturday morning. As promised, my instructions were waiting:

> *I'll call you at noon on Saturday, your time. Exactly ten minutes beforehand, I want you to do the following:*
> *1. Take off all your clothes and put on the Hello Kitty thong I brought from Japan last month. If you're cold, you may cover yourself with your*

bathrobe, but nothing else.
2. Place your hairbrush and hand mirror in the
middle of the bed.
3. Lie down beside them and wait, hands at your
side, until the phone rings. Then you may answer it.

That was it. A bossy to-do list. No loving endearments. No "can't wait to hear your sexy voice." None of the things a truly caring lover should say to his long-suffering and very horny girlfriend.

So why was my heart going pitter-patter in my chest?

Of course, I told myself, no man gave *me* "instructions." I'd play along because I had nothing better to do—for the moment. At the appointed time, I stripped and put on the thong, a black silk triangle on a string with a silly, beribboned kitty face on the front. I'd gotten a giggle out of it when he gave it to me after his last trip, but I hadn't worn it yet. It was a wise choice for overseas foreplay—definitely snug in all the right places.

But the mirror and the brush stumped me. Was he planning some kind of weird naked makeover session? I suddenly remembered some amateur porn pictures I'd seen on the Internet of a woman stroking her pubic hair with her hairbrush. She had this dreamy expression as if it were the most fascinating activity on earth, although at the time I suspected she was faking it for the photographer boyfriend.

Curious, I picked up the brush—screw the "wait with hands at your side" order—pushed down the thong, and ran it gently through my bush. No, I didn't blast off into orgasmic orbit at the first touch, but the sensation was interesting. Soft but rough at the same time, like the strokes of a cat's tongue.

The phone rang.

I jumped and tossed away the brush, as if he could somehow see me breaking the rules. It probably didn't help that I gulped, guiltily, in the middle of my "hello."

"Hey there, hot stuff, did you do everything on the list?" His voice was deeper than I remembered. And cocky. Too cocky.

"And what if I didn't?"

He laughed, warm and slow. "Then I guess I'll have to make you do as you're told."

"Sweetie, in case you didn't notice, you're thousands of miles away. How will you make me do anything? Not with words."

He paused. "We'll see about that."

In spite of myself, my cunt muscles fluttered, as if a secret butterfly was tickling me inside with its soft wings. But I didn't have to admit that to him.

"So, Part-time Lover, what am I supposed to do with the grooming implements?" I asked in my brattiest tone.

He laughed again, but this time he seemed embarrassed, as if he'd been the one caught with his hands down his pants.

"Well, I got inspired after I read that first e-mail. But I don't want to give away the surprise yet."

"Isn't it just like you to keep me waiting a long time for the good stuff?"

"Enough about me and my shortcomings, okay? I'd rather talk about you. Are you wearing the thong?"

"Uh-huh," I said, but with a healthy dash of defiance.

"Is it pulled up high so it presses between your pussy lips?"

That shouldn't have taken me by surprise, but it did, as a little zing of lust darted between my legs. "Somewhat."

"Pull it up a little higher. So that you can't think of anything else but that pressure against your clit."

I was about to refuse, on principle, but my hands seemed to reach down of their own accord and tug the sides another inch farther over my hips. An involuntary sigh of pleasure escaped my lips.

"See, that feels nice, doesn't it? Can you feel it rubbing against your sensitive pink asshole, too?"

His voice was so sweet it slipped into my ear like hot fudge sauce gliding over ice cream. Already my face was hot, partly because those dirty words were making me blush, partly because they were really turning me on.

"You didn't answer me," he scolded.

"Yeah."

"Yeah, what?"

"Yeah, it's rubbing up against my asshole," I murmured.

"Good. Now, I want you to open your robe and hold the mirror in front of your gorgeous breasts."

As I reached for the mirror, I noticed my hand was trembling. What would he tell me to do next? And would I continue to obey this easily, like a pliant little sex slave with no will of her own?

"Tell me, is your chest flushed and red, like it gets when you're all turned on?"

My "yes" slipped out before I could manage a lie.

"And your nipples? Are they hard yet?"

"Not really. The room's pretty warm."

"We'll have to do something about that. I want you to try a new trick. I want you to rub the mirror against your nipple very gently."

An unusual idea, but I figured it was worth a try.

I gasped as the cold, smooth surface brushed my areola.

"Does it feel good?" His voice had a hopeful lilt.

"Great," I sighed as I moved the mirror in slow circles over one nipple, then the other. "It's cold at first, but then it feels hot. And then it feels like your fingers are touching me there." Not to mention that the sensation of fire and ice was shooting straight to my pussy and making my hips do a twitching dance against the mattress.

Through the receiver I heard a little "hmph" of victory. "I'm glad it's working out so well. But I want you to stop now."

He couldn't mean it. This mirror trick definitely called for further exploration. "You're kidding, right?"

"I'm afraid not. But remember, all good things come to her who waits. I want you to move the mirror lower. To the kitty picture on your underwear."

I considered mutiny, but I had to admit that following orders thus far was bringing unexpected benefits.

"Okay, for this next part we have to get you wet. Very wet. But that shouldn't be a problem. I know how much you like to touch yourself."

"Yeah, and how about you?" I fired back.

"Guilty as charged, though I don't have nearly as many opportunities as you do, especially on the job. But right now I'm feeling fine—lying on my bed with my cock in my hand, a little lotion for lube, and a hot babe on the phone who sounds like she's getting hotter by the minute."

I frowned. For the first time he'd struck the wrong note. I couldn't help but picture him stretched out on a hotel bed, a blandly tasteful picture hanging on the wall beside him, pay-per-view porn on the TV. And the woman of his dreams on the other end of the phone was so far away, so insubstantial, she could be anyone willing to read the lines.

"Wait a minute, lover boy, before we proceed, what's your credit card number? Phone sex services always make you traveling businessmen pay up front to play out your fantasies, don't they?"

He was silent for a moment. "You are making me pay, babe, don't doubt it for a minute." The satiny seducer was gone. He was himself again. Lonely and a little sad.

"Hey, I'm sorry. I know I'm being a bitch, but it's tough for me."

"Yeah, I know. It's not easy for me either. Listen, I want to make you happy. Can you let me try? I know it's just words."

I felt another twinge, but higher this time, near my heart. He was trying, I could tell. In bed, in the flesh, he was more a man of action than words, but his new tongue technique was surprisingly effective. "It is making me happy. Really. Now where were we? I believe you were about to order me to masturbate."

His laugh was mixed with a sigh of relief. "That's exactly what I was about to do."

"I need very specific instructions, though. I promise to be a good girl and do everything you say."

"Hey, if that's what the lady wants. So, why don't you spread your legs for me? But just a little. Now I want you to touch yourself through the thong. Rub your clit until you make a nice wet spot on the kitty."

The hot-fudge voice was back, pouring down my spine, pooling warm between my thighs. My finger pushed the silky cloth of the thong back and forth over my sweet spot so deliciously I moaned into the telephone.

"Are you watching yourself in the mirror?"

I gazed down at the reflection of my finger wiggling away. Through my lust-fogged eyes, it looked like a stranger's hand, as if another woman were making love to me. The thought made my breath come faster. "Yes, I am watching."

"It's the best sight in the world, isn't it? A horny girl touching her pussy. But you have to take your hand away now."

I wailed in frustration. "Not again. Come on, I was just getting into it."

"Trust me," he cooed. "You're going to like this next part. I want you to give your clit a spanking. Not too hard. Just a few slaps to teach it a lesson for being so ravenous."

With a soft cry of shame, I covered my face with my hand. I suddenly felt so exposed, as if he'd reached through the phone and pulled me open to discover something darker and more secret than naked flesh. As if he heard that little voice deep inside me whispering, *Yes, you do deserve a spanking for being so hungry for sex. You love it when he makes you do bad things, so you can do just what the teacher wants and be good and bad at the same time.*

"It sounds like you're ready to begin. Shall we?"

Panting, I brought my flattened fingers down against my mons, once, twice, three times, groaning as the sharp jolt on my clit rolled through my whole body in waves.

"Again," he commanded.

I slapped myself once more, whimpering until the hot prickling pleasure faded.

"Very good. Now, we've got one more thing to try. I want you to pick up the brush, push the thong to the side, and press the end of the handle gently against your vagina."

I caught my breath.

"Um, I'm not so sure I can do that." My voice squeaked out, small and scared.

"What's the matter?" he asked, confused. "Don't you ever put hard things inside when you play with yourself?"

Should I tell him the truth? That, sure, I could talk like a crazed nympho, but when it came to push and shove, I was a pedestrian masturbator. Too chicken even to put my own fingers inside. "Actually, I don't."

"Hmm, I wouldn't have guessed that. Could you be a brave girl and try? For me?"

It really was magic the way he made his voice so warm and soft it sank under my skin to melt every muscle in my body. Including my tongue, which babbled out the answer I wasn't sure I wanted to give: "Yeah, sure. You know I'll do anything for you."

With a shaking hand and the help of the mirror, I guided the handle of the brush to my pussy lips. It probably helped that my only companions were his words, whispering inside me like the echo of my own lust. I don't think I could have done it if he'd really been watching.

I pushed the end of the brush slowly inside. My swollen lips parted with a faint, welcoming smack. He had made me wet with his talk. Very wet. I pushed deeper. The handle slipped all the way up to the point where the brush flared into bristles. It looked silly, but it felt nice. And very naughty.

"It's in."

"Good girl. You don't know how jealous I am of that lucky brush. But now we get to put everything together for the grand finale. Do you think you can come around the brush if I let you play with your clit and rub the mirror on your nipples?"

A rhetorical question if there ever was one. I was certainly willing to try. I had to clench my legs together to keep the brush in place, but the rest was easy. He was right, too, it was magic how it all came together. The mirror was his one hand, twisting and tugging my nipples. The thong was his other, teasing the groove of my ass. The brush was his cock, so hard, so *there*.

And all around were sounds, moans and rhythmic grunts racing at the speed of light under the Atlantic, the squish of a lubed-up palm on his cock, the click of my finger finally snaking under the thong to bare, slick flesh.

"Tell me when you're going to come. I want you to come now," he barked.

"Yes, now," I called out, just as his guttural cries shot back through the phone.

I could hear it was as good for him as it was for me.

Afterward, he told me how much he missed me and asked, uncertainly, if I missed him, too.

I touched my fingers to my belly. I was a little sore down there, deliciously tender and used. As if he had just been inside me, as if he still was there, filling me with his voice, his cock, his love. I wanted to tell him I didn't miss him at all, because he was with me.

All it took was words.

GALATEA BREACHED

Thea Hutcheson

I want to tell you about Frances Butler. She's just like Jean, my stepmom of high school and early college years, all carved and polished. I had been obsessed with her at one time. I never understood how such an elegant and idealized version of a woman in those tailored and fitted wardrobes moving with such studied and calculated grace could be, well, a woman, in the shitting and pissing and fucking way of women.

Watching Jean proved to be impossible. She had a sixth sense or some kind of radar that made her either see me or shut the curtains just in time to thwart me. For three entire days while I was a freshman in high school, after a long end-of-summer bout of B movies including *The Stepford Wives*, I'd thought that she was a robot. Jean was so not sexual for me. A lady, not a woman. I never got to ask my father before he died what he got when he married her, what that side of her was like. One of life's unsolved mysteries, I figured.

Then our real estate agent met Frances, who is an interior designer, on a job. She introduced Frances to our leads group last year. They've given each other a lot of referrals since then. I've used Frances to decorate the show models in the upscale housing I develop. She's got a good sense of design, which makes my work look better.

I noticed right away how much she resembled Jean and I wistfully figured this was another mystery I would never plumb. Frances is from the same mold, the same cut, the same jig as Jean. Yes, there's individual variation, but Frances is the same silver, tall, thin, austere, and graceful, still well-built woman in her late forties, an elegant and tasteful block of something, something impenetrable, impermeable. Or she was. Something happened over the holidays. It had been building since Thanksgiving and I had watched it with fascination.

She had left for the holidays and come back tan, sporting a kicky haircut, a less sculptured wardrobe, and missing her wedding ring. She laughed more and blushed often. She smelled of newly ripened sex under the White Musk she'd adopted. Pygmalion's Galatea had cracked, and the woman underneath the facade was steaming with sudden life.

What Pygmalion had broken her out of that hard shell, and to what goddess had he prayed for the favor, I wondered. What was such a favor worth? I know what I would pay to see her break. I also knew that the first blush of warmth had not been followed up. The predatory way she appraised the male market at the monthly socials our leads club hosts was a neon sign flashing and I wasn't sure if the men were blind or afraid.

It was kind of sad, in a way, because of her breeding. I wondered how she would manage to get a guy for more of what she'd been given in the hot nights wherever she'd gone for the holidays. So, she'd been stewing in her own juices all this time.

This early-summer day was beautiful and my office was only a few blocks from the restaurant, so I walked to this month's social. I was heading up Cartwright Street when I saw Frances on the opposite side of the street. She was looking at the early-nineteenth-century houses on her left.

I thought I would be sociable and cut across to walk the rest of the way with her. She stopped suddenly and I slowed, staying behind her without hailing. When I got up behind her I saw what had transfixed her. A man was leaning against the side of a turret on one corner of the house as a woman sucked his dick.

Frances was enthralled. This is why I like to watch. There was an entire subtext in her posture, her aura, which told me that what had happened to her had been an awakening by someone else rather than a waking on her own. Yes, I gloated, no tenderness; her ex-husband's sweetness had won her originally; I'd heard her say so. No, the touch on her had been that of a wild and passionate artist.

I watched Frances take in this guy now. He was well built, his muscular arms bent, his hands fully spread, threaded through the woman's thick hair. His head was thrown back and his mouth was open, loose, angelic, but I saw the wrinkles deepen around his eyes and his head tilted just so. The play of tension in his forehead told me every stroke of the woman's tongue across his flesh.

I was getting a hard-on when I looked back to Frances and noticed the fine beading of sweat on her graceful forehead. The sunshine reflected off it, giving her a sheen. She took in the sight of the man receiving pleasure and she was that woman giving the pleasure. I could see her place herself there, telling herself, "This is what I looked like doing it to my lover." She lifted one hand toward her breasts—a dove sliding home. It hesitated, not landing, and I was drawn to the soft cleavage where the silk dipped down into a V.

Galatea was breached and yearning, I thought, alive with golden warmth. I wish I knew who'd opened her, the Pygmalion responsible for this bit of magic. The man was coming now, grunting deeper with each stroke. The woman was taking it in marvelous form. As he wound down, I took a last look at Frances. She looked hungry and confused.

Hurrying back across the street, I went on to the corner, where I crossed. I looked down the street at her. She had just turned to continue walking and I waved cordially. She gave me a hesitant wave back. I chuckled all the way through the door.

I ordered a drink and went to work. I gave a few referrals and shook a bunch of hands, introduced people. Many of the people were here at my invitation. I bring people together. People live in my developments, and that means a steady stream of people wanting something.

I'm good at watching, spotting trends, connections, juxtapositions. You want someone? I just happen to know him or someone who knows her. You need something? I know someone who has it. And people remember that networking with referrals of their own. I give, they give back, I gain. Nicely elegant.

I looked back a little while later and there was Frances chatting with her friend the real estate agent and the owner of a window cleaning business at their usual table. I wondered if she told any of them what she'd been watching. What did they do when they went out, just the girls, since her divorce?

A sultry voice hit my ear the same moment the musk hit my nose. "You look good tonight, Dick . . . son."

God, my cock rose to say hello before I could. Camille Stuart sold Internet access. She also sucked dick. She had this way of going down really slowly, oh, so slowly, your cock sliding down her throat like it's heaven and then—bam, she pulls back really fast and hot damn! your cock is down her throat like greased lightening. I swear the first time she did it I came, straight shot right to her belly, and she took it, took the whole thing and asked for more.

"What'cha doin'?" she said.

"Just thinkin'." At that moment, I spotted Greg Johnson across the room.

She giggled and ran her fingers down my back. My dick jerked as I thought of those fingers. "I like it when you think, Dickson."

"Yeah, that so?" I said.

"You think the most dee-light-ful things." She jiggled and her breasts brushed against my back. "Tell me what you're thinkin'."

I smiled. This could be interesting.

"I'm thinkin' that after a while you and Greg are going to go back to my place and have a little party in the bedroom. I got a new camera set up in there. I'll join you later."

Camille could see Greg over my shoulder across the room. He sold T-1 phone lines and they'd had more than referrals between them since I'd introduced them. She smiled and tilted her head at me. "Okay. It's been awhile and his new goatee looks so wicked."

I gave her a key card with a code on it. She kissed me on the cheek. "See you."

I made the rounds after that, keeping an eye on Frances. She met mine across the room and for a moment I could see the hunger, the yearning there. I wanted to read it, gather every bit of meaning I could, and lay it over my curiosity about Jean like a blanket so I would see her true shape. I nodded to Frances. Sometime later, she tapped me on the shoulder.

"Good evening, Frances," I said as I shook her hand. The light-green silk was attractive on her tan and contrasted nicely with her silver hair. It wasn't just the candlelight. She had a high color and was more animated—coming less from afar like my stepmom, Jean, and more warmly immediate now. Maybe it was a couple of glasses of wine, maybe it was her awakening.

"I wanted to say thanks to you before I left," she said. "The last two leads you gave me were very good." She was standing close to me. I let her, turning slightly so that I was more in her space. Then I said, "You're leaving?"

I caught Camille's eye and nodded to her. Camille smiled and waved bye-bye.

I turned back to Frances. "Damn, I've been meaning to catch you, Frances," I said, smiling at her. "My aunt died and she left me a piece of art that's supposed to be Beatrice Wood's work. A bowl. I'd like to see what you think of it."

"Wonderful. I'd be delighted. Give me a call this week."

"Well, I only live down the street a block or so. I thought maybe that you'd come up tonight and see it."

From the way she paused I could tell that she wondered if I was beginning a seduction. Funny, she'd always acted like she disapproved of my wild bachelor ways before.

She kept it safe, ladylike, from habit and inexperience. "You live in this part of town?"

"Yeah, it's handy and good advertising to live in your own developments."

"Okay. Let's go."

"Give me a minute to say goodbye to a couple of people."

Ten or so minutes later, Frances and I walked out the door together. The moon was nearly full, and its light made her hair shine argent and turned her tan the gleaming buttery color of electrum. The air was still warm, and a light breeze made her nipples rise up under the now silver-frosted silk.

All the walk home to my loft, I could tell she could feel my presence, was tasting it as she wondered what would happen when I got her there. I let it build, sliding into her space, brushing her arm occasionally as we walked.

I opened the door for her, and she was watching me when I turned around from closing it. Her eyes shone in moonlight, filled with a need she couldn't name but she thought I was going to tear out of her soul. I was, but not the way she thought.

The bowl was in the study. I motioned for her to follow. The TV's writhing colors lit the room. Frances turned to the source of the light. Camille was sucking Greg's dick dead center on the big plasma screen. It wasn't deep throat, but he was sure diggin' it. Frances sucked in her breath and I shrugged my shoulders.

"What can I say? She likes to be watched. She says there's

something sexy about it, but I know she likes the camera more. It's always watching, but is someone watching it? She can only wonder..."

Frances dragged her eyes away from the screen and tried to look at me. Her hand caught halfway to her breasts again, the dove caught at the door. What had he given her there? Her eyes crept back to watch as Greg moved behind Camille to put his finger between those tender, swollen lips.

Her back dipped, that creamy ass went up in the air, and I swear Camille's hips spread so wide I could see up her swollen cunt. I have never seen any woman so eager for whatever a man wanted to do. He gave her two fingers and played her clit with his thumb. The squishy noises set a brisk rhythm.

Frances said, "I think I should go."

This was not what she expected, and she really wanted me to make her stay but was too much the lady to say it. Well, this once, I would make it easy. I picked up the remote and zoomed in. Greg slapped Camille's ass lightly and she moaned. She settled lower as she offered herself up to him.

"No," I said, pinning Frances with a stern gaze. "She wants us to watch. It's her gift and her deepest desire. You see, Frances, how he touches her in the most intimate ways, taking the gifts of her flesh, her pleasure?"

Greg continued to spank Camille, and Camille began to make noises deep in her throat after each smack.

"He'll spank her until her flesh is hot and then he'll fuck her, pressing up against that smarting ass. Every time he touches her will be a shock, a little zap straight to her clit."

"He'll come inside her, or maybe he'll pull out and come on her breasts. And she'll do all this on the off chance somebody might wanna watch."

I waited, as each of Greg's perfectly placed strokes heated Camille's bottom. He swore there was no one more fun to spank. Frances was transfixed, so I zoomed in on Camille's ass.

"See how artfully he works her? He knows what he's doing. Each stroke is a judicious application of pain with exactly the right amount of sexual stimulation to push her pleasure where he wants it."

"You're the audience she craves, Frances. She doesn't know it's you. It could be anyone, but it's you. He creates the art, you fulfill her fantasy."

Frances never looked at me. She stared, mouth slack, while Greg made Camille ready. Did she see herself writhing under the ministrations of her artist lover? Her hand hovered, just out from her breasts, and I wondered again what the dove had found there.

I could imagine that district attorney husband of hers fucking her coldly, frozen in moonlight. Her lover had been the sun, glowing hot after a few glasses of wine, a heady French kiss.

"He'll make her come now and you'll witness it." I accepted her paralysis as complicity and zoomed out as Greg mounted Camille.

He slid in slowly, pulling on her hips at the top of the stroke to seat himself. She flattened her chest on the bed, offering everything to his long, thick dick.

The camera allows me to watch from any angle, any position in the room, and I watched Frances as I panned the camera around so that we had a side view of Greg fucking Camille. She cried out every time he stroked. Camille likes to make a lot of noise.

Frances's face was shiny with sweat. Her eyes were big and her pupils were dilated. She was breathing shallowly. *Galatea pressing against the ragged edges of her shell.* Every time Greg slid in I imagined all that desire straining to get out of Frances.

"Please, Greg, get it. Get it. What can I do so that you can get it better?" Camille's face was flushed, her mouth red and swollen.

"Lift, baby, lift, I'm almost there," Greg moaned. "Can you feel me knocking at that door? You're so wet. Yeah, that's it, here I go. Oh, Camille, baby, I'm fucking you good."

Frances was swaying a little on those high heels. I stepped in behind her. "Do you see how she likes it? She can hear the camera pan. It's not just that Greg is pleasuring her, it's that she knows we are watching her in her extremity."

Camille was weeping. "Yes, you're in all the way, you're getting it all. Fuck it, fuck it."

Greg reached around her hip and I knew he was playing her clit. "I'm coming," she moaned, and Greg began to fuck her hard, grunting with each stroke. "Ah, take it, babe, take it, here it comes." The final throes of his orgasm drove him into her and he stayed in freeze-frame for a long moment.

He finally patted her on the ass and she sank down with him on top. When he rolled off, she turned over. Her blonde hair was in disarray; her breasts scratched and chewed, her snatch moist and shiny. She laid a finger across it idly and dipped between her lips to come up with a glistening finger. She brought it to her lips and sniffed delicately before licking it.

Frances sighed and turned. "I really need to go." Galatea breached, confused, yearning for complete release.

"Well, thanks for coming over," I said. "I know Camille appreciated it. I hope you enjoyed it."

Frances practically ran toward the door in her haste to get

out. I closed it. I realized that she never saw the bowl. That's okay. I'll ask her back.

I know a Pygmalion, Pygmalion Jones. He's an artist who's been after me to find someone to look at his etchings; real business coupled with a real come on. I'll give him the referral to Frances in a few days, after she's had time to think. Back when Frances was new to the club, Jones and I had a drunken discussion about her, about my stepmother, Jean, and the possibilities for more earthy behaviors from their hard-shelled ilk.

When he sees Frances's name, he'll remember more than the mammoth hangover the next day. When he meets her, he'll recognize Galatea and he'll take her into the hot light of his sun. And I'll be watching from the loft above his studio to see why the dove does not nest, Galatea extricated completely from her shell, and Jean's earthier womanly aspects revealed for the benefit of my teenaged curiosity—vicariously after all these years—a fair deal all around, I'd say.

In the meantime, there was Camille, just now warmed up. I picked up the remote and panned to the table next to the bed. Yes, the bag of tiny clothespins was still there. I put several CDs in the player and went to join them.

Because, you know what I love about networking? Givers gain.

CALL ME

Kristina Wright

Claire dialed the number before she lost her nerve. The phone rang and she switched hands to wipe her damp palm across the sheet.

"Hello?" It sounded as it he'd just woken up.

"Hi," she said, trying for a sultry voice. "It's me."

"Bad connection," he mumbled. Static crackled across the line.

She frowned. That wasn't what he was supposed to say. She tried again. "I've missed you."

"You have?"

"Yes. And this is an obscene phone call."

"Really?" he sounded more awake now, but not quite himself. "Sounds intriguing."

"Mmm...I promise you won't be disappointed."

"Well, sweetheart, where do we start?"

Something wasn't right. The static on the line made it impossible to hear him clearly. "Sam, let me call you back. This is a lousy connection."

"Who's Sam?"

"Oh my God—" It wasn't Sam. She had just propositioned a stranger.

"Hey, no, it's okay," he said quickly. "Don't hang up."

She hung up.

Claire stared at the phone, waiting for it to ring. She shook her head and picked up the receiver, carefully dialing the number Sam had given her. The phone rang twice.

"Change your mind?" There was humor in his voice. Humor and a warm familiarity that reminded her of late-night radio deejays.

"I'm sorry," she managed to say. "I'm trying to call someone else."

"So I gathered."

"My boyfriend, actually."

"Lucky guy."

"I'm sorry," she said again, feeling like an idiot. A horny idiot.

"I'm not." He chuckled. "So tell me, do you make a lot of obscene phone calls?"

She laughed. "Hardly. This is my first."

"You mean we're still on?"

"What? Oh, no, I meant I was trying to make my first one. I botched it, huh?" She absently rubbed her fingertip across her nipple. It was puckered, rising up from her breast. She stroked the opposite nipple until she had a matching set.

"I don't know," he said. "I'm willing to give it a go."

"Really? Do you get many obscene phone calls?" She

smiled, wondering what he looked like. She decided it didn't matter. She liked his voice.

"Actually, I'm hoping this will be my first one."

"Please tell me you don't have a sleeping wife or girlfriend lying next to you."

"Well, I do have a girl next to me, but she's a ten-pound ball of fur."

"Cat or dog?"

"Cat. Please, no jokes about men with cats."

"No, no," she said quickly. "I think it's sweet."

"What can I say? I like a little pussy."

She laughed at his lame joke. "You're cute."

"You don't know that. You haven't even seen me."

"True," she agreed. "But you sound cute. You sound…"

"Sexy?"

"Yeah, you do. Very sexy."

"Mmm…you sound pretty sexy yourself," he said. "What are you wearing?"

She laughed. "Is that a standard question with men? 'What are you wearing?' Why does it matter?"

"I don't know. I want the visual, I guess." She could almost see him shrug.

"Would you be shocked if I told you I'm naked?"

"I'd be aroused."

She kicked her legs out from under the sheet. "Well, I'm naked."

He groaned. "Well, I'm aroused."

"But are you naked?"

There was some rustling and then finally, "I am now."

"Are you touching yourself?" she asked, shocked at her own boldness.

"Oh hell. I wasn't, but now I want to."

She stretched out on the bed, phone cradled between the pillow and her head. She closed her eyes and imagined she could see this stranger with the sexy voice in front of her. He stroked himself up and down while he watched her. She slid her hands over her body, tugging gently at her nipples, caressing her breasts and stomach for him. She spread her legs a bit and felt the cool air glide over her fevered crotch. She gasped.

"What is it, hon?"

"I spread my legs. The air feels good."

"Are you wet already?"

"I haven't touched myself yet," she confessed.

"Are you playing with your breasts?"

"Mmm, yeah." She rubbed her fingertips lightly over her nipples again. "They're so sensitive."

"Pinch your nipples for me," he said. "Tell me how it feels."

She grasped her nipples between her fingers, as he requested, and pulled on them. She felt a corresponding tingle in her clit. "Oh god, that felt nice. I could feel it right between my legs."

"I bet you're soaked. I wish I could see you."

"Tell me what you're doing."

He laughed, a breathy sort of laugh that let her know he was aroused. "I'm running my hand up and down the shaft, slowly. Up over the head, then back down. Real slow."

"You like it slow," Claire said. "I like that."

"Yeah? I'd love to touch you like this, this slow. Run my hands over your body, so slowly until you begged me to be inside you."

CALL ME

"Mmm…" she breathed into the phone, hearing an echo of herself. Instead of being embarrassed, she was decidedly more aroused. "I'd like that."

"Touch yourself for me," he murmured.

She slid a fingertip over her engorged clit and gasped. "Oh, I'm so wet."

"Beautiful. Show me how you get yourself off."

Claire slid two fingers inside herself. She was so wet she was sure he could hear her. "Oh," she whimpered, using her thumb to rub her clit.

"That's it, hon." His husky voice urged her on. "Fuck yourself."

She could see him, see his cock. She whimpered. "I wish you were here. I wish you were inside me."

"Me, too. I'd slide into you slowly so you could feel every inch of me." His words teased her, driving her higher. "I want to feel your wetness around me. So tight and warm."

"Oh god. I want you to fuck me hard." She arched her back off the bed and raised her hips as if to meet his thrusts.

He groaned. "I'd fuck you hard. I'd bury myself so deep inside you."

She slid a third finger inside herself, wanting to feel it just as he described it. She moaned, pumping her fingers into slick wetness while she rubbed her clit faster. It wasn't her fingers she felt as the pressure built, it was him.

His breath quickened and she knew he was close. Her cunt clenched her fingers. She wanted to come with him.

"Oh! Yes, now, please! Come inside me," she moaned, thrashing around on the bed, fucking herself the way she wanted him to fuck her.

"Oh god," he gasped. "That's it, yes."

She could almost feel him throbbing inside her. She bucked against her palm, coming hard, riding the wave of her orgasm while his deep moans filled her head.

Her fingers slowed as her orgasm faded. Her cries became soft coos of pleasure as she teased her sensitive clit.

"That was nice," she whispered. "Thank you."

His quiet chuckle tickled her ear. "I should thank you. What a great way to be woken up."

She felt the postcoital pull of sleep and yawned.

"Tired?"

"Mm-hmm." She yawned again. "Sorry."

"Don't be. I'll take it as a compliment."

She smiled in the quiet darkness of her room. "I don't even know your name."

"Oh, I don't know if I can tell you that. It seems so…personal." They laughed together, then he said, "Michael Rossetti."

"Hello, Michael." She hesitated. Did she dare give him her real name? It hardly seemed to matter. "I'm Claire."

"Sweet dreams, Claire."

"You, too. Good night." She hung up and untangled herself from the sheets and hung up the phone. As tired as she was, sleep was a long time coming.

It seemed only minutes later when the phone startled her awake. She pushed her hair out of her face and fumbled with the receiver. " 'lo?"

"Good morning, sleepy girl."

She glanced at the clock. 7:45 A.M. "Hey, Sam. What's up? How's your trip going?"

"I'm fine. I was worried when you didn't call last night."

"I'm sorry, sweetheart. I tried to call, but I think I wrote the number down wrong," she said, feeling only a fleeting sense of guilt.

"That's all right. I'll send it to you in e-mail later. Everything all right?"

"Fine." She yawned. "But I need to get in the shower. I'll call you later, okay?"

"Sure thing. I love you."

"Love you, too." No sooner had she hung up than the phone rang again. She picked it up and said, "Forget something?"

"You've got the wrong person again."

A shiver danced up her spine. "Sorry, Michael." His name slid so easily off her tongue. "I wasn't expecting to hear from you."

"Amazing thing, Caller ID. I hope you don't mind."

She shook her head, amused and turned on at the same time. "Seems only fair, since I woke you up last night."

"Busy?"

She looked toward the bathroom. She needed to take a shower and get dressed. She was supposed to be in a meeting at nine-thirty. She snuggled back under the covers and spread her legs. "Not really."

"Good. Because this is an obscene phone call."

PLAY SPACES

Scarlett French

We dressed carefully, you and I. You couldn't
decide which shirt—the blue or the burgundy;
I fussed over whether to wear a corset or a
simple silk slip, eventually deciding on the sensual choice. The attention to detail, of course,
provided a distraction from our nervousness
about the evening ahead. We finally finished
dressing and preening, and pulled on our
coats. The cab we'd ordered honked from the
street below, and we scurried out the door.

You say it was my suggestion, but I say it
was at your instigation. However it happened,
we found ourselves being delivered to a cata-
comblike address near London Bridge. As we
climbed from the cab a slight panic rose in me,
but a thrill too, at the anticipation of what lay
in store for us. You seemed calmer, but when

you turned and smiled at me I saw that you were apprehensive too. Neither of us had been to something like this before.

We entered and showed our tickets, then were directed to push our way through plush red curtains to a cloakroom area where we deposited our coats and bags. As I straightened up from adjusting the straps on my heels and smoothing my slip, I caught you looking at me with a shine of pride. I smiled at you, gorgeous in the blue shirt you'd finally settled on, your hair brushed back but falling forward in that accidental way. You grabbed my hand, a little too tightly, and we proceeded through another pair of luxurious curtains.

On the other side, an extensive bar served several alcoholic drinks from huge bowls in addition to the usual beer, wine, and spirits. We ordered a honey punch each, then stood, sipping with an affected nonchalance and watching, like so many others. This was the neutral zone. We saw many people relaxing on sofas, getting into the feel of the evening before heading through to the other rooms. You looked to me to check in and I nodded that I was fine. Erotic images faded into one another on several wall-mounted screens, setting the tone. We saw a couple of people drift off in the direction of the rooms, so we downed our drinks and decided to follow them.

For the most part, the dimly lit rooms ran off a central corridor, allowing for exploration while reducing the foot traffic of people simply passing through. Jazz electronica played softly throughout the play spaces. We went into the first room. As our eyes became accustomed to the dark, red ambience, we noticed three people in the corner on a collection of huge satin-covered cushions. Watching them, I saw that there were two women and one man. They were writhing about and getting into another position, having obviously been playing with each other for a while. As we continued to watch, one woman lay back in the pile of cushions and spread her legs. The other woman buried her face between the first woman's legs and began to lick her, while swaying her ass in the air. Behind her, the man grabbed a condom from a box on the wall and rolled it over his erect cock. He entered her very slowly, guiding his cock in. As she continued to go down on the woman in the pillows, the man began slowly thrusting behind her, his hands firmly gripping her hips. All three were sighing with pleasure. I felt you grow hard behind me, your erection throbbing against my barely covered ass.

Against the other wall, a couple were touching each other, evidently inspired by what was happening in the corner. I had never seen anything like this before, never been in the same room as other people having sex. I was so wet you could have fucked me right there, standing behind me. You could have lifted my slip and entered me, and I would have been utterly ready. I backed up against your crotch so you'd know, but you leaned forward and whispered, "I suspect we could stay here all night, but let's see the rest of the rooms first and then decide where we want to be." I hated to wait for pleasure, but I had a sense that you were probably teasing me now to heighten it later, so I agreed.

We slipped from the room and headed down the corridor. Exploring the other rooms, we found a variety of sex acts going on. In one room, a man was being mercilessly spanked with a wooden paddle by a woman wearing a rubber dress; in another, four people seemed to be licking each other in some kind of group tongue-bath activity; fucking was happening in most rooms in various positions. Throughout the play spaces, a scattering of single men were watching and jerking off. In a fur-covered room, a couple of women were kissing and touching each other, which looked like a lot of fun, but I wasn't sure I wanted to be the subject of some stranger's jerk-off session.

You and I stood against a wall and whispered our preferences to each other. It turned out that we both wanted to go back to the first room and make something else happen there. But I had also seen a room with a partition inside the door and a sign that read, "Women-only space." A smaller sign below read, "For breast appreciation."

"Would you mind if I take a moment?" I asked. You smiled and kissed me, displaying another side to the trust between us. I kissed you back deeply, playing my tongue against yours, and drifted beyond the partition to the women-only space, our hands, then fingers, breaking contact at the last moment.

It was almost completely dark in the women's space except for tiny pink lights twinkling on the walls. With only silhouettes visible, I felt hands brush against my body as I walked further into the room. As my body was touched and hands traveled up to caress my breasts, I reached my hands out too, feeling a firm, slight body, then a softer, curvier one, feeling breasts of different shapes—through satin, through silk, and bare. A finger curved over my nipple, causing a surge of sensation in my already very sensitive clit. I responded in kind to the breasts before me and heard a sigh of pleasure, knowing that upon leaving the room I would have no idea who I'd touched, or who had touched me. My pussy clinched at the thought. I moved in further, making my way slowly around the darkened tangle of women, my nipples leading the way.

When I rejoined you, you whispered that I looked flushed, that you could see I enjoyed my time in the women's room, that you wanted to play with me now, bury your face in my luscious pussy, fuck me, make me come. I took your face in my hands. We kissed for a long time, drinking of each other. I wondered why we ever stopped kissing each other like this when we got home from work. Your kisses were magic and never failed to warm me up, even after a bad day. We held hands and walked back through to the first room, dancing our fingers on each other's palms as we went. Once back in the first room, we settled on a pile of cushions in the corner opposite the man and two women. They were languid now; sipping drinks and lying across one another, talking softly and laughing.

The music had been changed to a breathy, rhythmic tune which fitted the mood perfectly. I snaked my hand along your leg and up to your cock, which was rock-hard and faintly pulsing. I began to rub at your crotch, contemplating what I'd like to do with you, but I felt suddenly self-conscious and looked around to see if anybody was watching. A man had sat down in the center of the floor, cross-legged. He was masturbating slowly but seemed to be in his own world, taking in the sensual environment rather than anything in particular. A couple stood in the doorway fondling each other, but they were watching everything in the room, not just us. I relaxed a little and turned back to face you.

"You okay?" you whispered to me.

"Yup, and I want to do this. How about you?"

"What do you think?" you whispered, your eyes pools of desire.

"I believe I was here," I said, as I placed my hand back on your hard bulge. You sighed and your pelvis twitched upward.

My pussy began to clinch with want—we'd been waiting for this all evening. You wrenched open your button fly and yanked your trousers down to your thighs. Your cock sprang out in the process, then stood erect and perfect in the half-light. I straddled you immediately and slipped my tiny silk undies to one side, preparing to sink down on your cock and envelop you inside me. You reached forward to steady me, then brought your hand under the silk top that covered my thighs, providing some degree of modesty in this rather unusual situation. You reached your hand up and slid your fingers over my slippery clit, flicking gently and rhythmically, making me spasm softly and cry out. With your other hand you rubbed my nipples through the silk, each in turn. I couldn't help but pant, and as I vaguely surveyed the room through the pull of desire, I saw that several people had gathered to watch. Though less brazen a show than the earlier performance by the three in the corner, we were a show nonetheless. Unexpectedly, I found myself turned on now by the attention. I didn't want to be approached, but I found I did want to be watched. I looked at you and, reading me, you gave me a knowing smile, delighted by my change of heart as I hovered above you.

As you brought your fingers to your mouth and licked my juice from them, I heard a sigh behind me. We smiled at each other then, and I raised myself up, reaching back to steady your cock from its base. I moved your dick back and forth over my clit and wet hole until the head was covered with my juice. Around the room, I heard other slippery, rhythmic sounds. I was so fucking horny—and I was even more excited by the thought that I too was performing in this symphony. Deliciously slowly, I finally slid down, enveloping your shaft in my hot, throbbing pussy. Both of us took sharp intakes of breath until I settled down at the base of your cock and rocked back and forth a little to find the right angle. As I lifted myself up for the first time, then plunged back down, I felt you raise my slip so that those behind us could have a clear view of our fucking. I felt my pussy engorge further around your hard cock and juice streamed from me, making my thighs slippery. Your thrusts felt like heaven. In response, I brought my chest down to yours and stuck my ass right up in the air so that the audience behind us could get a proper porno view of your meat filling my cunt. I could hear the panting behind me increasing, just like my own, and yours. I loved this display—who would have thought I had an exhibitionist in me? I reached around and played with your balls while sliding up and down, building my orgasm. From the sound of your cries, your orgasm was building too.

It was a reminder of how much sex can be in the mind. This position was built for observation more than pleasure, and we would never have done it at home, but here in these rooms, it was the payoff to get the thrill of exhibitionism. I wanted people to get off watching us fuck—it made me feel sexy and powerful and even generous.

I heard an orgasmic sigh alongside us and turned to see a man standing nearby, a beatific smile on his face, among several others who had ventured closer. Noticing now that quite a crowd had gathered, some of whom had peeled off to be sexual together, I felt myself being pulled toward our orgasmic finale. I dropped the exaggerated position as I began to realize that there was something genuine and sexually honest happening in this room. From the beginnings of arousal, nervousness, and then performance, something organic was happening with this group of people. I knew then that I didn't need to objectify myself, or our sex, in order to participate, to feel sexually powerful, to be desired.

You must have been watching me, because you reached up and stroked my cheek, ever the listener—even of my thoughts. Our sex took on a more intimate tone, though it still felt welcoming of our observers. We slid against each other and I rocked and rocked on you until I felt my orgasm begin and spread in my belly. When it came it was surprisingly gentle, yet deeply moving. Yours followed immediately; you always get off on me coming. We held each other for a long time afterward.

Eventually, we drifted back through to the bar. For us, the rooms were somehow more the domain of anticipation than languidness. We had agreed on the need for some space now, and a cooling drink. A bartender brought over two extremely tall glasses filled with vodka, fresh lime juice and muddled mint. The ice crackled as I sipped, contemplating the evening.

"I can't believe what we just did," I said finally, flush-faced and a little proud.

"I can," you said, grinning, making circles on my thigh with your finger. The expression on your face became pensive then. "We're so lucky to have each other." Your eyes had that earnest look that makes me want you.

"We sure are, lover," I smiled. "Tonight hasn't just been a horny evening—in a way it's revealed what was already there between us."

"Exactly!" you exclaimed, "And that is why we're lucky."

"Then take me home for more," I purred, holding your gaze.

You didn't need to be asked twice. You stood and offered me your hand. The diamante buckles on the ankle straps of my heels sparkled as we crossed the floor and disappeared through the plush curtains, heading for the coat check.

VOICE OF AN ANGEL

Teresa Noelle Roberts

Jessie was hired for the costuming job at the
Berkshire Opera because she had a great port-
folio and several years of theatrical costuming
experience.

Her knowledge of opera, however, was limited to what she'd learned from classic "Bugs
Bunny" cartoons.

It didn't really matter for the job. As long
as the directors could explain their vision for a
production and point her in the right direction
for visual inspiration, she didn't need to know
that much. But plunging into a new world full
of beautiful but unfamiliar music had piqued
her curiosity. Most people in the company
were glad to answer her questions, but she'd
found a particular friend in the set designer.
Nelson, a fiftyish self-described "flamboyant

opera queen," was delighted to have someone new to convert to his passion, and she often found his nonmusician's explanations more comprehensible than those of the people with conservatory degrees.

So it was to Nelson she turned when the early discussions of a production of Handel's *Giulio Cesare* left her confused. "I have no problem with crossgender casting. If the director wants Nora Murray to play Ptolemy, I'm glad to make the costume. But aren't they going to have to transpose the part for her?"

"A lot of the Baroque repertoire is written for a castrato voice. Yes," Nelson continued, seeing her wince, "it means exactly what it sounds like. Disturbing thought, but supposedly it produced a lovely voice, high but powerful. Mutilating boys for the sake of art is frowned on nowadays, though, so women usually get those roles."

"If it's a choice between cutting some poor kid's balls off or making someone built like Queen Latifah look manly, I'll take on the extra costuming challenge."

"I'm glad that's your department, not mine—talk about engineering! On the other hand, I do envy you getting to fit Daniel Gwynn."

"The one coming up from New York to play Caesar?"

"A countertenor, and one of the best. A male alto or soprano, to oversimplify vastly," he added, seeing the blank look on her face. "They're rare, of course, and great ones rarer still, but Daniel sounds like you'd imagine an angel would, and he's utterly gorgeous to boot. The idea of getting paid to have your hands all over that man and maybe see him in his underwear...my dear, I am terribly, terribly jealous."

Jessie immediately imagined some pretty, fey, androgynous

creature, Boy George with more class. Nice to look at, fun to costume, but not her type. Just as well, really.

When Daniel Gwynn actually walked into the first cast and crew briefing session, though, he wasn't at all what Jessie had imagined. For one, he was tall, six-two or six-three if she estimated correctly (and after several years of fitting bodies of all shapes and sizes for costuming, she usually did) and nicely built. He wasn't a broad-chested fantasy figure off a romance novel cover, but lean and leggy and gracefully strong like a great cat, not at all the androgynous sylph she'd pictured.

He wasn't pretty, either, but handsome in an almost stern way, all about high cheekbones and chiseled features and pale gray-blue eyes that looked cold and remote until he smiled. He was dressed all in neutral colors—black jeans, charcoal gray sweater, lighter gray turtleneck under it to protect his throat against the chilly spring air.

When he smiled, his severe good looks were transfigured into something otherworldly yet very sexy, something like the way she'd always imagined Tolkien's elves (the cute college boy appeal of Orlando Bloom notwithstanding). Jessie melted—right along, she figured, with everybody in the room who fancied men. His speaking voice astonished her even more than his looks: rich, resonant, lower than she expected.

"Aren't you a countertenor?" she blurted out when they were introduced. "I'd expected your voice to be higher." Then she bit her tongue, realizing that she'd sounded like an ignoramus.

He gave her one of those blood-igniting smiles. "Only when I want it to be," he replied in a much higher register, still backed with all the power of years of vocal training. "My natural speaking voice is lower than my singing voice," he added, in the deeper tones she'd heard at first. "That's not uncommon."

She felt herself blushing. "I'm sorry. I can't believe I said that. I'm new and still have a lot to learn. The regular members of the company are used to my dumb remarks by now, but I should have spared you."

He laughed, and even though Jessie was convinced, after her faux pas, that it was at her rather than with her, it was still a glorious sound. "Don't worry about it. You're a costume designer, right?" he said. "I don't understand how you do what you do, either—I'm color-blind, I've got the design sense of a wombat, and I can't sew on a button—but I do appreciate someone who dresses me up and makes me look good." He winked. "I'll look forward to chatting with you more during fittings. Maybe you can finally teach me to sew on a button."

Then he wandered away to talk to some of the other singers, leaving Jessie still flustered and repeating to herself firmly that the wink meant absolutely nothing. She would not, repeat would not, get a crush on him, although he was just as good-looking as Nelson had claimed.

She managed to keep that resolution for a couple of days.

Then she actually heard Daniel sing.

As the costumer, she wasn't expected to attend most rehearsals, but in the early stages, when the company was still working out its vision of the production, she found it useful to sit in on a few before she got too committed to costume sketches that just wouldn't work. Besides, she was intensely curious about this particular production, and, to be honest, about what a countertenor sounded like.

She scrunched down in the front row of the theater—forlorn and curiously stale-smelling now with no sets, no costumes, no special lighting—prepared to take notes on any costume ideas that popped into her head. In Handel's day, it was perfectly manly to wear brocade and lace and accepted practice for heroes to be played by high-voiced castrati, but in the twenty-first century the male soprano emperor and the female Ptolemy had a hip, gender-bending quality, at least on paper. Might she be able to work some of that contradiction into the costuming?

As soon as Daniel began to sing, though, she understood there was no real contradiction.

The story was purely a coat hanger for the music, the glorious music.

And the music was designed to show off a voice like Daniel's.

He sounded as otherworldly as an angel, yet sensuous. She'd heard boy sopranos singing in a similar range, but their voices were light, innocent, almost disembodied. Daniel's voice was definitely bodied, and in a pretty damn amazing adult male body, and although it didn't sound "masculine" in any of the ways she was used to, it unquestionably was. That should have seemed weird, but instead it was hot, as if he were turning the whole notion of gender on its head in a way that made Jessie even more aware of his body and hers.

This music didn't carry the raw emotion of some of the nineteenth-century opera she'd gotten to know earlier in the season, let alone the gritty, let's-get-down passion of rock. There was no mess involved. It was all about technique and elaboration. Yet its beauty, and the implausible glory of Daniel's voice, seemed to go straight between her legs and vibrate.

As she sat transfixed, listening to that gorgeous voice coming from that gorgeous body, Jessie could feel her nipples
perking. Her labia were swelling, throbbing, pressing against
the seam of her jeans, and she could feel her panties getting
sticky.

Male yet not male. An emperor yet a soprano.

She would dress him in lace and brocade, drawing on the
wildest extravagances of the Baroque era, but in a way that
showed off the strength and power of his body. Make the
breeches the more fitted ones that became popular shortly
after this opera was written, to show off his long legs; make
the coat really full-skirted and over-the-top—maybe a loud
but glorious brocade lined with Imperial purple—but make
sure it emphasized his shoulders.

And Nora...Nora and the other women playing male roles
would dress like Baroque drag kings, with obviously padded
crotches, and blatantly fake mustaches and goatees. Make
them all strange and beautiful, partaking of both male and
female, to support the beauty of the music and play up the
aspects to that a modern observer seemed strange.

As she made notes, Daniel kept singing and she kept getting
wetter.

As she began to make some sketches, Daniel and Fritz, a
baritone, had a brief song exchange.

She'd always liked Fritz's deep voice, thick and golden
as caramel syrup, but with Daniel's angelic tones weaving
around it, soaring and trilling in ways Fritz could not, it
sounded grounded, mundane. Just a guy after all, though a
guy who could sing better than most men could dream.

The director came forward. "Thanks, Fritz. Daniel, Mei, I
want to hear your first duet now." Mei Wong, who was playing

Cleopatra, stepped forward, looking even tinier than she actually was next to Daniel's height.

Jessie set down her pencil and closed her eyes to listen. She'd been wondering about the romantic duets, how the two voices would blend. Until she'd actually heard Daniel, she'd thought the two high voices together in a love song might seem strange, at least to people who weren't aficionados of Baroque opera. She wanted to hear Daniel and Mei together the first time without visual cues.

Shame not to see Daniel, though, she thought as they began to sing. It must be his good looks that were affecting her so.

It wasn't.

If anything, the voice's soaring beauty seemed even more striking without his face and body distracting her. And the way it wove in and out with Mei's—astonishing! They were roughly in the same range, but with entirely different timbres to their voices.

It was as if Mei was being courted by a beautiful being from another world. Love among the aliens.

Make that lust among the aliens, because if anything the duet was tickling her clit more than the solo had. That voice...that voice!

Jessie opened her eyes to see Daniel gazing down at Mei. He wasn't trying to act the role yet and didn't look particularly romantic or lustful. (To be honest, Jessie wasn't sure where the opera picked up the story. Was this even a love duet or was Cleopatra saying something more to the effect of "Get out my country, you great oaf of a Roman"?) But she still envied Mei for being the subject of his attention, his gaze.

His singing.

Jessie shifted in her seat, bit her lip to stifle a moan. This was more than she could stand. Quietly, she gathered her things and crept away to the bathroom.

Safely in a locked stall, Jessie peeled her jeans down, leaned on one shabby gray stall wall. One hand slipped between her legs.

She was slick as a seal, hot as an oven, and all without being touched.

She couldn't hear Daniel's voice from the bathroom, but with the memory fresh in her ears, it only took a few flicks of her fingers against her swollen clit to bring her over the edge.

Music soared in her head as she clenched on herself and muffled a betraying groan.

Afterward, as she zipped up her jeans and composed herself, Jessie scolded herself for being even sillier than a teenage girl lusting after—whoever teenage girls lusted after these days. (Justin Timberlake? Aaron Carter?) For heaven's sake, she was supposed to be working with Daniel Gwynn. Costuming him. Dressing him up to be even more striking than he was in street clothes. Measuring him. Fitting him. Touching him.

Curiously, while that thought gave her a pleasurable shiver, it was didn't compare to the thought of hearing him sing again.

Jessie tossed and turned that night, Daniel's voice echoing in her head, enough to inflame her. Finally she grabbed her favorite vibrator, hoping it would end her torment.

As soon as she turned it on, though, she knew it wouldn't work. That whirring noise—it was so ugly, so intrusive, drowning out the sense memories of Daniel's singing.

Disgusted, she shut it off and went into the living room,

rummaged around until she found some CDs Nelson had loaned her that, as yet, she hadn't had a chance to play. He hadn't had *Giulio Cesare,* but he'd passed on another Baroque opera, *L'incoronazione di Poppea,* by Monteverdi.

She skimmed the liner notes, figured out who the counter-tenors were, and selected an aria to put on repeat.

Then she settled back on her comfortable couch, spread her legs, and imagined Daniel.

Oh, this voice wasn't quite right—glorious, but not quite right. For all she knew, this singer was better. He was someone famous, after all, someone who'd sung at the Metropolitan Opera and La Scala, not the young, up-and-coming talent that Daniel Gwynn was.

But he didn't have the same effect that Daniel did. She felt a thrill of pleasure listening to the music, but an aesthetic thrill, not a sexual one that helped with the throbbing frustration between her legs.

Finally, she cursed and got the vibrator. It wasn't what she wanted, wasn't what she needed, and its noise fought with the strains of the music, but its familiar shimmering touch stirred her. That, and the music, and the vision of Daniel worked in concert. (Luckily, the upstairs neighbor was away and the downstairs neighbor worked the night shift, or she might be the first person ever to get the cops called on her for playing Monteverdi too loudly.)

If Daniel were here now, singing for her, he'd get quite a show, she thought. What would he think if he saw her like this, naked and splayed-legged on the couch, a vibrator pressed against her clit and two fingers working in and out, moaning, "Sing for me, Daniel"?

Would he like her breasts with their tidy maroon nipples,

the line of her hips, the wet sheen of her shaved pussy?

She could picture those pale, astute eyes studying her, and felt herself flutter in response to the idea, one step closer to coming. Would he like what he saw? No way of knowing, but hell, it was her fantasy.

She imagined him stopping in midsong to enter her, imagined Daniel's face, his hands, his cock—his voice in her ear, making sweet music of her name.

And with that, she exploded.

The next day, Jessie sneaked a small tape recorder into rehearsal and taped Daniel.

The sound quality was ghastly when she played it back at home. It sounded as though he was singing five miles away through a pair of old socks. Unaccompanied and unmiked, he was scarcely audible. Yet every night, she played it over and over again, coming and coming.

Thus armed, she was able to maintain some kind of professional demeanor during the preliminary work on Daniel's costume, although it certainly wasn't easy. Daniel smelled good, a bit musky, a bit like raw silk, and like the big, handsome cat he was, he seemed to enjoy being the focus of attention while he pretended to take it all for granted. Jessie's skin pulsed whenever she got near him, but she took a deep breath, looked ahead to an evening with her vibrator and the recording, and tried to think of it as particularly torturous, drawn-out form of foreplay.

It worked until it came time to perfect the fit for his satin breeches. Doing the muslin for these had been trying enough, but she'd had an intern with her then, writing down measurements, handing her safety pins and chalk, asking questions, and generally forcing Jessie not to give in to the temptation to make a pass at him. (Jessie was half-convinced that Ayesha knew that her distraction value was higher than her value as an assistant that day. Some of her questions were too dumb, and some of her timing was too handy, to be entirely artless.)

But Ayesha had the flu and had been out for most of the week already, and the older Polish woman who also helped out in the shop had been called away for a family emergency. They were already a little behind schedule—what else was new?—and finally, she decided to go ahead with this, the third attempt to do Daniel's fitting. It was definitely easier with help, but she had to get on with things.

Even if it meant being alone with him.

On her knees in front of a man she lusted after, separated from his flesh only by a thin layer of fabric that she would be tweaking so it fit snugly. It wasn't just that she would be able to touch his thighs, his glorious butt; she was obliged to touch them in order to get her job done.

Jessie's heart was racing as if she'd gulped down four double espressos in rapid succession, and her stomach jittered to go along with it. She was one Daniel-smile away from having the shaky hands to complete the too-much-coffee illusion, and that, considering that she was working with pins, would just be bad.

And, of course, he had to say something. "You seem a bit anxious, Jessie. Is anything wrong?" It was hardly sexy banter, but in Daniel's amazing voice, it was good enough, or bad enough.

Some adolescent bit of her thought, *He cares. He cares enough to notice!*

Her nipples perked up. Her clit quivered. And predictably, her hands started shaking.

"I'm fine," she lied. "Late night, last night, and a little too much coffee this morning, that's all."

"Good. I think I'm nervous enough for the both of us."

"You'll be great," she replied. "And I'll make sure you look fabulous, which should close the deal. The big companies will be beating down your door after opening night." While the Berkshire Opera didn't have the fame of some of the big-city opera companies, it was watched very closely by those same big companies. Making a splash here in a leading role could take Daniel from up-and-coming young singer to—would a male diva be a divo?

He gave her a devastating smile. "Thanks, Jessie. That helps."

Something about the way he said it suggested it hadn't helped enough. Oh well, he knew she was hardly an expert on opera, and what nervous performer ever listened to a mere costumer about their worth anyway? Their fashion statement, maybe, but not their worth.

The only way Jessie was going to survive this fitting was to pretend that Daniel was a mannequin. No more talking, she vowed. In silence, she went to work, smoothing and stroking the satin of the breeches against his legs, marking with chalk where she'd need to adjust the fit. She focused on the luxurious, smooth fabric, trying to shut out the heat of his body, the scent of his skin.

It might have worked, too, if she hadn't needed to double-check that she'd gotten the placement of the buttons at the fly just right.

She'd been trying desperately not to look there, but she had to check—it would hardly do for the breeches to fit perfectly everywhere but there. And when she did, she saw Daniel had a hard-on.

A hard-on that suggested if his voice hadn't been pure gold, Daniel could have found work in the porn industry.

A hard-on so nicely outlined by the tight, slightly stretchy fabric that she could see the mushroom shape of the head, even the way it was throbbing. The buttons were straining, and she was pretty sure he wasn't wearing underwear under the breeches.

That explained the nerves: he was also concerned about getting through this very intimate fitting.

There was only so much a woman could take. Jessie set down her pins and chalk, took a deep breath and reached out. "May I?" she breathed, and Daniel nodded frantically.

Her fingers fumbled at the buttons, and she cursed the impulse that made her use this historically correct but currently inconvenient closure, instead of something more expedient, like a zipper. (It wasn't as though it would show much under the voluminous coat!)

Then she forced herself to slow down and to make the best of necessity by playing with the teasing possibilities. With each button, she paused for a few seconds, stroking at the little bit of him now revealed, driving them both a little crazier.

By the time the breeches were open, though, Jessie was done with playing. She took him in her mouth.

He groaned, a deeper, more animal noise than she could have imagined him making, even in her wildest fantasies. She could already taste a bit of precum, salty and delicious. He was thick as well as long, not a candidate for deep-throating, but great to play with. She closed one hand around his base and began to stroke in time with her sucking, cupping his balls with her other hand.

Her sex was flooding. Lovely as it was to have him in her mouth, she wanted him inside her, fucking her. In a little while, she'd probably beg for it. But not yet. Now she was just enjoying the taste of him, the way he stretched her mouth a bit.

His balls tightened under her hand. "If you don't stop—" he choked out.

She backed off but left her hand hefting his balls. They felt so right, there. "Thanks for the warning. Not that I'd object to you coming in my mouth, but I'd had other hopes for that cock of yours."

He grinned, not the practiced performer's smile, but the cat-with-the-canary smirk of a man who'd stumbled into sex he'd hoped for but hadn't really expected. Then he caught her up and gave her a kiss that tickled down and touched places that shouldn't have been reached by lips and tongues coming together.

Even while they kissed, she was peeling out of her clothes. The yoga pants she favored for crawling-around-on-the-floor days might not be elegant or sexy, but they had one advantage under the circumstances: they were easy to take off. Daniel's clothes were a little trickier, especially the still-basted breeches, but one thing she'd learned in her years as a costumer was how to help someone undress quickly.

Normally, Jessie would want more kissing, some serious time spent toying with her nipples, some reciprocation for her oral teasing. But she'd been fantasizing about Daniel for so long that she was wet and eager.

She looked at the project on the cutting table (one of Mei's gowns, a heavily boned confection of heavy gold-on-white brocade designed to look like something a person of Handel's era might imagine Cleopatra wearing) and was briefly tempted to sweep it onto the floor.

No, it would wrinkle, and expensive white fabric and floors were a bad combination. Dancing internally with impatience, she took a few seconds to drape it neatly over a chair, out of harm's way.

Then she hopped up on the table and lay back.

Proving his worth as a gentleman, he bent down to lick her, but she stopped him. "No," she muttered. "I want your cock. Please."

Again that smug grin.

Lucky guess. A table the right height for cutting wasn't a bad height for fucking either (provided, at least, you had a partner as tall as Daniel), although it took a little fussing to get everything properly aligned. The extra perhaps thirty seconds this took was excruciating, and when he finally pushed inside her, Jessie almost screamed with relief.

He filled her pussy the way he'd stretched her mouth. She couldn't move much in the position she was in, which was both exciting and frustrating. Exciting because it put her at Daniel's mercy, depending on whether he stroked in and out slowly or pounded to the finish line, and frustrating because, at the moment, he *was* stroking slowly. All right, she should give him credit for realizing that when you're well-hung, you need to take a little extra time and make sure your lover's opened up and ready for you. But she was ready, dammit, more than ready.

Jessie grabbed his ass with both hands. "Please. Harder." She pulled him forward as she did, pushed with her hips as best she could, trying to get more of him inside.

Daniel began to pump faster.

Yes. That was what she'd needed, a good, primal fuck, one that would leave her a bit sore afterward but right now felt really good.

Her abs fluttered. She could feel her pussy clamping down, making him feel even more deliciously huge inside her. Her nipples felt sharp and hard as blades. Yet she couldn't quite come. This was just the kind of fucking she'd thought she'd needed, and it felt great, but it wasn't quite doing it. New partner nerves, maybe?

She moved one hand to her clit, planning to give herself that extra little boost she needed to break the dam and let loose the orgasms she could feel were ready to pour out with a little more stimulation.

Just at that second, Daniel's eyes widened. He pumped into her wildly for a few seconds, let out a small sound of surprised pleasure—a much smaller one than she would have expected, given the power of his voice—and ground against her. She could actually feel his cock jump inside her as he came, a tiny but delightful movement that still didn't quite push her over the edge.

He spent about fifteen seconds looking happily dazed and smug before the smugness gave way to embarrassment. "Sorry. It's been a while and I've been thinking about doing this with you way too much lately, but that's no excuse."

"It's all right," Jessie said feebly, trying to be polite. Damn, and she'd been so close!

"No, it's not. I pride myself on a good performance." The stage smile again, but with a playful wink. "You wouldn't let me lick you before. Will you now? I'm told I'm quite good with my tongue," he added in a teasing voice. "I think it's from learning to sing in Italian."

Tempting. Very tempting. A few licks right now ought to do it, and she had no doubt that Daniel's tongue was skilled. But the mention of singing suggested another idea—one that the sudden contraction of her pussy told her was a good one.

"Would you sing for me?" Jessie begged. "Sing for me while I touch myself? Please? Your voice turns me on so much."

First Daniel blushed and looked bewildered, but another look, sexy and mischievous, replaced it. "Only if I can touch you instead. I want to feel you come on my hand while I sing for you."

Just the thought of it made her spasm a little.

He settled two fingers on her clit. Circling it gently, he began to sing.

His voice poured over Jessie's bare skin, caressed her all over, circled around her clit following his fingers.

She spread her legs wider, picturing the song slipping inside her—and jumped as Daniel's fingers slipped in instead. Still wet and open, and slick with his come, Jessie took his index and ring finger inside her easily. He seemed to know exactly where to touch, where her G-spot was, how fast to pump her (quick and forceful as industrial dance music), how much pressure the other hand needed to put on her clit (delicately, gentle as a waltz.)

Or maybe everything felt so right because his voice was also working its magic on her, intimate as his hands, yet impersonal as an angel on high.

He hit a particularly lovely high note and trilled it, a technique that she knew had a name if she'd had enough brain cells left to care. She didn't.

It worked like a musical vibrator.

Jessie contracted. Her hips bucked up, pushing herself harder onto his hands. The room spun as she cried out "Ohgodohgodohgod."

The orgasm was a long one, and he kept playing with that note the whole time. Finally she flopped back on the table, feeling, if not quite sated, then damn content.

He kept going, though. Kept singing. Kept touching her.

Suddenly she understood. He wasn't done with the piece of music, and if he'd finished prematurely before, he wasn't going to this time.

One of the things she'd picked up about Baroque opera was that an aria could be ornamented and varied for as long as the singer's invention and lung-power allowed.

She'd learned from sitting in on rehearsals that Daniel had plenty of both.

That was the last coherent thought she had for a while. Occasionally her brain would kick in long enough to admire some lovely trick of his voice, but then some equally lovely trick of his hands would set her coming again and her cries almost drowned out his voice. Or maybe it was the other way around, that she focused on the hands, but the voice triggered the orgasm.

She lost count at five, but it seemed that there were more.

Finally, she caught his voice faltering, at about the same time she was starting to get almost too sensitive. She grinned wearily, clapped, and croaked, "Bravo!" while pushing him gently away.

"What, no encore?"

"You need to save your voice for rehearsal later," Jessie said, amazed she could form so coherent a thought. "And I'm worn out. But I'd definitely like an encore sometime."

He grinned. "And to think," he said, his voice a little shaky, "that some people think Baroque music lacks passion."

PUFFY LIPS

Susie Hara

Elena sat at the bar. She so rarely drank these days that after just one martini she could feel the effects. The way it made her feel bigger than god. The way it took the edge off, loosening her tension and sharpening her sensations so that her whole being was ripe and extended in sensuous tentacles, like a cross between a mango and an octopus. Mangopuss. Or Mangopussy. There, she felt them, the lips of her mangopussy, large and puffy in her mind's sensometer. And then the image of her labia, puffy and pink and engorged, expanded through every cell, pore, and vein of her mindbody, with all the worker bees of her consciousness focused diligently on the task. One big Labia Majora Fest, big-ger even than the monthly ovulation brouhaha. *Labia Majora*, she thought, now that sounds like an exotic cocktail.

I'd like a Labia Majora with a twist, she said to herself. It would be sweet but not too sweet. Mango juice, a touch of cherry, a touch of orange, some soda water, swirls of cream, and something heavy-duty like Grand Marnier. Oh yeah, and a twist. Damn. She could market that.

She looked around the room. Men, they seemed like exotic creatures to her. See, this was what happened when she hadn't had sex with a man for a while. "Men"—perhaps a species of animal she knew from another lifetime. Somewhere inside her, she dimly remembered things about them—their hands, their lips, their tongues, their fingers, their cocks—even their minds. The memories stirred and lumbered out into the light, like a beast coming out of hibernation. It was just that she hadn't thought about men for awhile. Not in *that way*. She had temporarily put men out of her mind. She had been more focused on women. Maybe focused was not the right word. Obsessed. Feverish. Devoted. Prostrate, worshipping at the temple of the divinely honeyed cunt. But now. Now in the moment, here in this bar, Elena felt something in her blood. It was a need. A need for something meaty. Yes. *Meat.* That was it, exactly. She wanted man meat.

She looked over at a table of them, having a drink after work. There was one specimen who had this particularly meaty quality. His hands were meaty, his shoulders were meaty, but most of all, his chest. He had a meaty chest. She would like to knead it with her hands, rub her labia all over it, and lay her cheek down on it. Elena smiled. These were her requirements for the night.

She caught his eye. He let his gaze rest on hers for a minute, then he went back to talking to his companions. For a few seconds. Then his eyes returned to hers. She popped an olive in her mouth. She sucked on it. No chewing, no swallowing. She held his eyes with hers as she held the olive in her mouth. Then she licked her middle finger. Once. He raised his eyebrows a bit. And flushed slightly. Cool, but not *so* cool.

She made a big show of getting off the stool. Out of the corner of her eye, she saw him watching. She approached his table, then lightly touched his shoulder with her still-wet finger as she walked by. No eye contact. She left the bar and waited on the street, chewing the olive. She would give him thirty seconds. She started counting. One-one thousand, two-one thousand, three-one thousand. He came out of the bar at twenty-three. She smiled and walked around the side of the building. He followed. She went down to the end of the alley, by the dumpsters. No one was around. She leaned up against the building. She could feel the cool, hard brick through her blouse.

"Take your shirt off," she said.

"Oh, I see. Just—take your shirt off? No hello, no what's your name?" he said, a half-smile curving the corners of his mouth. He put his hands flat on her chest, just below her collarbone but above her breasts. And just left them there. She could feel the heat of his palms. And her nipples hardening.

"OK. Hello. Take your shirt off."

"I'll take my shirt off if you—" he moved his hands down her body and put one hand up her skirt "—if you take off your panties." He hooked a finger under the elastic. She drew her breath in sharply. He looked at her, eyebrows raised, waiting. She nodded. He pulled her pants down to her ankles. She stepped out of them.

He unbuttoned his shirt. Meaty. Just as she'd hoped. And covered with thick hair, like a pelt. Grrrrrr. He took off his shirt and dropped it on the ground. She kneaded his chest with her hands. She wanted him down, down, so she could rub her lips all over his chest. His meaty chest. She put her hands on his shoulders and pressed down. He smiled and went down, thinking he knew what she wanted, moving his lips up her inner thigh on his way to her puffy paradise.

But she had other plans. Her pussy lips were singing their swollen siren song, they were longing for the meaty-chest man, the he-man caveman hunter chest, covered with fur. Before he could move his mouth lips to her puffy cunt lips, she maneuvered herself down and commenced rubbing her wet labia all over his chest, his pecs, his nipples, his stomach. She was moaning a cavewoman's moan, a satisfied carnivorous wet woman's moan, as she slipped and slid on his warm terrain. He was breathing hard, smelling her and holding her ass in his hands, feeling her circular hip motions as she smeared him with her juices. She bent her knees more and stretched her hand down, down, so she could put her hand on his cock meat. She felt his cock, hard and alive, through the cotton cloth of his pants. It felt so good, so like home, like someone in the kitchen making her a nice big meal. Hello, she thought, hello friendly cock home-cooking man. He was moaning now too, inhaling her scent and rocking against her hand. Then he reached up with both hands and pinched her nipples. That was it. It put her over the edge. It surprised her, the way it happened so suddenly—usually with a man it took longer. She came in three short waves. She pressed hard into him so her pelvic bone and clit connected with his meaty chest. As the pulsing became less and less and she hung there, knees bent and breathing hard, the words came into her mind. *Two out of three of my requirements are met.*

She still had her hand on his hard cock. He hadn't come. She looked at him. He stood up and rubbed his knees.

"Ouch," he said. "My knees."

"Ug," she said. "You are such a caveman. Thank you." She tugged her skirt down. Then she hugged him, softly laying her cheek against his chest for a moment. She sighed. *Third requirement met.*

She kissed him on the forehead and walked away slowly, down the alley.

"That's it?" he called after her, putting on his shirt. "No flowers, no candlelight?"

She turned around, said, "You are the bomb. You are the best. That was just what I needed." And she walked backward into the night, still looking at him, a smile in her eyes.

He finished buttoning his shirt. Picked up her underpants and put them in his pocket. He looked up. She was still walking backward, her eyes resting on him, giving him that Mona Lisa smile. He watched her turn, round the corner, and disappear.

WORTH IT

Alison Tyler

As the ring slid onto my finger, I knew it was all over. The sparkle of diamonds glinting in the dim candlelight. The pink tourmaline shining like a flame. Those jewels foretold our demise as clearly as any fortune-teller could have. I knew the end was inevitable, even if I didn't know why. Well, that's not altogether true. I knew, sort of. I knew in a half-assed, bitchy kind of way.

A week before, Byron had taken me on a dream shopping spree to Tiffany & Co., had told me to choose the ring I desired the most. "Go for it, Gina. Pick out the one you love." What girl wouldn't melt at an opportunity like that?

Flustered, flattered, I'd landed on this one after nearly an hour of breathless searching.

Or, at least, one damn near like it. Dramatically dark pink stone in the center, two perfect diamonds on either side, a classic platinum band. Admittedly, the price was astronomical, but Byron had the money for the ring. And I was worth it, right?

Apparently not.

This ring did not come in the pretty pale blue box that makes all women's hearts skip a beat, but in a knockoff lavender velvet container, from a knockoff jewelry store in West L.A. *This* ring cost five hundred dollars instead of twelve thousand dollars. And I should have been happy with whatever Byron gave me. I know that. But like a bossy five year old who throws a tantrum at her own birthday party, I was not happy at all. Because it was clear to me from the look in his watery green eyes as they carefully appraised my reaction that I wasn't worth it.

Like I wasn't worth a lot of things.

I wasn't worth kissing in public. ("PDAs are *so* revolting.") I wasn't worth risking potential shame or embarrassment in the back row of a movie theater. ("*Stop that*, Gina. People might see.") I wasn't worth trying something new in bed, even though Byron had dabbled in adventurous sex with girls before me. But no matter how I cajoled, he wouldn't travel uncharted territory on our California King.

Velvety handcuffs? No.

A leopard-print blindfold? No f-ing way.

He'd had *anal* sex before me, twice, with a girl he met in New York City. I knew this because early in our relationship, when we'd been in that cozy sharing place that happens prior to going long-term, he'd confessed. I'd told him that I'd lost my virginity to a frat boy whom I chose to do the honors because he put his arms around me on a balcony during a party to keep me warm. Chivalry had gotten him where no man had before. We retreated to my dorm room twin bed and he'd made me come twice while sixty-nining.

Byron had countered with his tale of debauchery in New York City. He'd bragged about the act, as if it were something he did every day. But as the story continued, I deduced that playing this way had been entirely the girl's idea. He'd simply gone along with the concept, taking down her jeans, bending her over the hotel bed, fucking her *there*. I don't actually think he enjoyed the act—too dirty for Byron, who liked things antiseptically clean, from missionary-style sex in our king-sized bed to the grout between the white tiles in the bathroom. Still, he held the experience close to his heart, like a badge of courage. It was a medal of sexual adventurousness for a Boy Scout like him.

Whenever we made love after that, I thought of the girl. She had blonde hair, cut short and spiky. She wore sunglasses even inside, and she liked to chew Double-Bubble gum. There were pictures of her in his scrapbook, black-and-white photos of her blowing bubbles, of her winking at him, of her with her hand in the belt loop of her jeans, looking oh so cocky.

What did she have to look cocky about?

Simply this: she'd had Byron in a way I couldn't.

In truth, I hadn't had sex like that with anyone. I was only nineteen. My experiences were limited. Even frat boys who are willing to sixty-nine for hours don't always broach the taboo topic of anal sex. I wished I'd done it, though. Knowing that Byron had ass-fucked someone else made me feel uneven with him, as if he were winning. As if he'd *always* be winning.

So I asked him to do it to me. To take down *my* jeans. To bend *me* over.

"Uh-uh," he said, shaking his head. "You won't like it."

Why? Why wouldn't I like it?

"It'll hurt."

"We can use K-Y."

"It's—it's dirty, Gina."

He said the word in a way that made me know he thought *dirty* was bad. But to me, the thought of getting Byron to do something dirty couldn't have been sexier. Mess him up. That's what I wanted to do. Rumple him around the edges. Untuck the hospital corners on his highly starched personality.

"Come on," I urged him. "You've done it before. You know how."

"Kiddo," he said in his most condescending voice. "Trust me. It's not for you."

Byron was nearly thirty. You'd have thought he would enjoy introducing me to new things, but aside from training me in which brands he preferred for toothpaste (Crest), mouthwash (Scope), and soap (Dial)—the types his mommy always bought—he claimed that he wasn't much of a teacher.

Yet I desired knowledge. I craved experience. Now that Byron wouldn't even consider having anal sex with me, it was all that I wanted. I started to think about my ass in a way that I never had before. To consider my behind as a sexual object in its own right.

Although I'd always been in favor of hipster panties, or (at the skimpiest) bikinis, I now bought myself a rainbow of thongs, and I twitched my ass in them when I walked, feeling that ribbon of floss tickling me with every step. Opening me up.

When I took a shower, I took great pleasure in using the pulsating massager between my rear cheeks rather than over my clit. The rush of water there had me breathless and shaking as I'd never been before. And when I touched myself solo, I'd finger my ass simultaneously, and my orgasms intensified in ways I'd never imagined. Nobody had told me. Nobody had explained.

Maybe, I thought, Byron needed to see what it would feel like. Maybe nobody had told *him,* either. The next time we made love, I tried to touch him back there, but he swatted my hand away, and the lovemaking stopped abruptly. How could I consider that? How could I dream he'd be into *that?* When I went down on him soon after, something he *did* like, I tried accidentally-on-purpose to kiss him back there, slipping lower between his legs than normal, but he pulled me back up to his cock, horrified that I would even consider rimming him.

The more he denied me, the more I craved what I couldn't have.

How strange that something I'd never known I wanted now consumed me. I dreamed about him taking my ass. I wanted him to pound into me. I felt as if I were on fire all the time, felt as if the curves of my ass were a beacon, a neon sign, pulsing. Throbbing. And was I just imagining things, or were other people suddenly realizing how cool my ass was? I wore tighter jeans. I wore shorter, flirtier skirts. Byron's best friend, Joshua, seemed to notice. On a day when I wore Daisy Duke cutoffs, he couldn't keep his eyes off me. But Byron was oblivious.

I was determined to wake him up.

Whenever I felt the mood was right, I'd try to perk Byron up to the concept. I'd ask him to play with me the way he'd played with Vacation Girl, the trippy little blonde-haired minx in the Vuarnet shades who'd let him take her from behind.

But what did I know? Maybe she'd taken *him.* Maybe she'd fucked him from below.

"Come on," I begged yet again one evening after a party. We were both tipsy, but I acted a little more drunk than I really felt. "Come on, Byron, let's try it."

By then he knew exactly what I meant. We'd had this conversation often enough for him to know what "it" was. His face squinched up. He shook his head. He looked as if he'd just taken a bite of something rotten.

"I want to," I told him, giving him my most desirous look. Lashes fluttering. Bottom lip in a bitable pout.

"No," he said, in a tone that let me know he was gearing up for a fight. "No way."

Although I hadn't given the concept of anal sex much thought before Byron and I got together, now I had discovered that I really *did* want to. Men had been complimenting my ass for years. Since high school, even. Boys who suddenly realized that they weren't breast men, but ass men, took an extra look at my derriere when I walked by. Did anything come between me and *my* Calvins? That's what the boys wanted to know. Byron had that ass in his very own bed, and he wouldn't glance at it twice.

How crazy it is that I begged. How pathetic that I had to go that low.

He'd fucked *her* that way. It was all I could think about. *She* got him to do it. She wouldn't take no for an answer.

I got drunk again. Drunker this time. But I was prepared. I'd purchased a bottle of glistening lube. I unfurled a fresh towel and spread the blue terry cloth out on the bed while Byron was in the adjoining bathroom, brushing his teeth. My body, ass included, was squeaky clean from a shower. I was

Crested, Scoped, and Dialed, as tempting as I could possibly manage. Somewhere in the back of my head, I knew that most men would have dived at the opportunity of doing me the way I craved. Young chicklet on the bed, ass up, ready for sex.

Byron said no.

He didn't want to do the act with the girl he would marry. That's what it all came down to. He tried to make it seem as if he were sparing *me* an indignity. Really, I could tell the truth was a different story entirely. I wasn't worth it. The fight that followed was groundbreaking. Byron didn't like me arguing with him about anything, and he punished me by leaving the apartment, storming out to have a cool-down walk in the night air.

All by myself, and drunker still, I looked at the photos from his vacation in New York, the one he'd gone on with Joshua after finishing graduate school. The one where he'd met the girl. I saw her gazing from under her shades, saw her daring me.

I took that dare.

What I did was indefensible. What I did was wrong, wrong, wrong. What I did wasn't actually a *what* but a *who*—Joshua Sparks, Byron's best friend.

I didn't start up with the "fuck my ass" request immediately. I simply began responding to the flirtatiousness in Josh's dark brown eyes whenever we were together. I held his interested stare a beat too long. Whenever we talked, I put my hand on his shoulder, or thigh, or the inside of his wrist. At parties, I stood too close. At dinners, I always sat across from him, and my stockinged toes did naughty things between his legs from under the table.

Josh started calling when he knew Byron wasn't going to be around. "Hey, Gina, is Byron there?"

"No, Josh."

"Good—"

He wanted me to talk dirty to him when he was at work. "Tell me what you want," he'd demand. "Tell me everything."

"You first," I'd counter.

He wanted me to watch him jerk off.

I could do that.

He wanted me to give him a blow job in his car, during rush hour.

I could do that, too.

He wanted me every which way he could get me. At least, that's what he promised. "Every which way—and then all those ways again."

But would he fulfill my one true desire? That was the question. Or would he make me beg the way I had begged Byron, my fingers on the split of my ass, ready to open myself up to him? Would he make me beg, and then reject me? I didn't think I could handle that.

When Josh and I finally got together after all those months of dancing around the issue, I didn't know how to ask. I simply rolled over in bed and bumped him from behind.

"Byron won't," I told him. "I've asked, and he won't."

"Why not?" His strong fingertips lingered between my ass-cheeks. He touched me more firmly and I shuddered all over. "Why, Gina?" I looked at my ring, glinting at me accusingly from the bedside table. I looked over my shoulder at Josh. "Why do you want to so bad?" he asked, amending his original question.

"Because he won't." I'd built the act into something else in my mind. A super hurdle. Something to overcome.

Josh didn't want me to see it like that. He wanted me not to get over it, but to revel in every single second. He didn't want me to beg him to fuck my ass, he wanted me to beg him not to stop. He explained this to me as he touched my naked skin, humbling me with the sensation of his fingers spreading me apart. Making my heart race faster as he inspected me. And suddenly I didn't want him to fuck me there just because Byron wouldn't. I wanted him to fuck my ass because I needed him to. I wanted him to drive inside of me, to make me scream, to make me feel as if he were fucking me all the way through my body.

Josh knew what he was doing. There was plenty of lube and there was lots of stroking. He slid in one finger. Then two.

"Oh, yes," I sighed. "Oh, Josh."

He finger-fucked my ass as he rubbed my clit with his free hand. My body responded instantly. I felt the wetness spreading down my legs as my pussy grew steadily more aroused. He dribbled the shivery cold lube down the split between my cheeks until it rained onto the crisp sheets. He made me come before he even brought his cock to my hole. He made me come again with only the very head of it inside of me.

"Oh, god," I murmured, undone by the feeling. "Oh, fucking god—"

He kissed the back of my neck as he worked me, and when he slid in all the way, I bit into the pillow and cried.

Byron was wrong. Yeah, it hurt, but it hurt in the best way possible. It hurt like nothing else ever had, and the pleasure of being filled was like no other experience. I didn't want it to stop. I didn't want it to end.

I thought about Byron denying me this. I thought about the spiky-haired blonde and her "I dare you" stare. And then I came again, as the diamonds made dizzy, drunken rainbows from my knockoff ring on the bedside table.

I tried to make myself feel bad for leaving Byron. I told myself I ought to have at least a twinge of guilty conscience over it. But the truth is this: he simply wasn't worth it.

ANIMALS

Rachel Kramer Bussel

"I want you to hold me down and fuck me
hard. Don't treat me like myself, or like a
woman at all—treat me like an animal,"
I told him, the last such pronouncement I
would make. Aidan was the kind of guy who
always made me feel depraved, and he had a
special knack for making my pussy tighten so
fiercely I worried that it would stay that way
permanently, the way parents warn their kids
their eyebrows will stay furrowed if they keep
on frowning. I'd been lusting after him for
almost a year, but had finally broken through
my own fear and told him what I wanted
from him, only to find he felt the same way.
I'd never asked anyone anything of the sort—a
little spanking, a few minutes of bondage, a
few dirty words thrown my way, but that was

about it. This was different. This was real, raw. That's how much I wanted him. At first, I wasn't sure if he got what I was saying—I didn't want him to hold back, *at all*. I could tell that he had been holding back, just enough to make me long for more, to make me feel slightly put off, as if he thought I was too fragile to take what he could really give me.

Maybe it's because, outside the bedroom, I'm his boss at our small town's indie record store. I'm the girl all the wannabe guitar players drool over—five-nine, long jet-black hair often tinged with green or red, eyebrow ring, purple lipstick, powder-pale face. My clothes, some mixture of black, tight, and sexy, usually paired with imaginative stockings and combat boots, never fail to make at least one set of eyes turn at the store. But Aidan, unlike most of the guys who passed my way, caught my gaze immediately. He was smart, not just some snot-nosed punk looking to steal CDs when they thought I wasn't looking. Aidan could talk as easily about Dorothy Parker or Bukowski as he could the Buzzcocks or Braid or even the Beatles. He didn't lord his intelligence over anyone there, either, it just came out if you provoked him enough and stayed hidden, like a turtle under its shell, if you didn't. He was more clean-cut than the other guys, so you had to peer a little more closely to see his edge, to catch a sneer or raised brow, to see the smirks that were gone almost before they'd even formed. He had plenty of scars and dreams and fantasies, but they were wrapped up so tight I didn't know if he'd be able to let go, even though it was clear from his rock-hard cock and the look on his face, eyes half-lidded and wet mouth slack, that he wanted me.

I was sick and tired of lying back and letting some guy rock his cock inside me as if we were on a seesaw, gliding gently upward, pausing, then zooming downward at the most predictable pace imaginable. Even at twenty-five, I knew that sex should take you out of the everyday, should make you as wild and ferocious as a rabid dog—in heat. The guys before Aidan had been cute enough, but they just couldn't give me what I most craved, what I dreamed about, squirming against my slithering fingers as the walls of my bedroom shook with the latest single the store had sent our way.

"Are you sure that's really what you want, Tina? You already drive me so crazy with that sweet ass of yours, twitching it the way you do when you walk, like you're moving each of those cheeks separately, taunting me with them so I just want to grab you and smack them till they're bright red." Just hearing the normally sly, sarcastic Aidan saying those words, thinking those thoughts, made a tiny trickle of liquid slide down my thigh. Since somehow finding ourselves wedged together behind the counter last week during closing, we'd been fucking like rabbits until every moment seemed suffused with his scent, his touch. Even when we weren't together, my pussy was working overtime, as if asking when he'd be back.

We were standing in the doorway of my tiny kitchen, part of the so-called bargain I'd scored to live in the East Village, meaning I got a minuscule doll-sized set of three rooms, rammed right up against my neighbors' identical layouts. But I didn't care, because how much room did I really need to get fucked into oblivion?

Aidan was behind me, his back against the front door, while mine was slammed against his hard cock. I could feel it pressing between my ass cheeks as I pushed back against him, and I leaned down, showing off my flexibility by wrapping my wrists around my ankles, making my already short black latex skirt ride up my unusually bare thighs. I was sure my tiny, wet red thong barely covered my pussy lips. He growled, and I knew I had him right where I wanted him. He tugged upward on one side of the thong, making it dig into my cunt lips until I whimpered, tears of joy forming in my eyes. *More,* I thought, *I want more.* Then he let go, but immediately grabbed my hips and slammed me hard back against his dick. I heard the metallic twang of his zipper being undone, and then his warm cockhead was tracing the contours of my slit, tapping against my opening as if he was testing out the right key to unlock my door. Except Aidan knew after only a week together that he could have me anywhere and everywhere, could take me when I least expected it and I'd be wet and ready for him. He was simply that kind of guy. Just as I was getting used to the feel of him rubbing against me, making me ache more than I would have thought possible, he stopped.

He pushed me roughly forward, and I had to scramble to place my hands on the floor in front of me to steady myself. Then he shoved the remaining fabric of my skirt well over my hips and reared back, slapping my right ass cheek hard. The sting traveled throughout my body, seeming to leave my mouth in a whoosh of air. I had to really focus not to tip over, and then he did it again, the sound echoing through the room. He tugged on my thong, harder this time, keeping it there so it bisected my lips, letting them fall on either side of the thin piece of fabric. "You want me to treat you like an animal, T? I hope you're ready for me." *I am, I am,* I mouthed to myself.

Then he let out a growl, mimicking several animals at once as he brought his hand down and spanked me again, this time using his hand to get at both cheeks at once. He leaned down, and before I knew what was happening his teeth had sunk into my skin, the fleshy underside of my ass, his mouth moist, his teeth sharp as I got what I'd asked for, got the fangs and claws as his nails dug into me, his teeth nipping down my ass to play at my thighs. When he moved us into the other room, carrying me over to the bed and laying me down on the mattress, my body pressed flat against the crisp sheets, all of me bared, open, waiting, I sneaked a peek behind me and almost didn't recognize him. Like the best actors, he'd become someone else, gone to his own primal core as he scowled, his features contorted into a wild snarl of pleasure and passion and lust and sadism, his eyes sparkling with excitement as he whacked my legs apart. I went limp, a willing rag doll, as he pounced on me. His weight pushed me deeper into the bed, his cock pushing against my slit.

I felt deliciously, delightfully small, a little girl to his huge-ness, as his hands raked through my hair, then clawed down my back, the red lines burning as he did his best to mark me, brand me his wildest animal. He reached beneath me, pinch-ing my clit hard, until it hardly even felt like my special nub, but something else entirely. He ground my hard pink button between his fingers, so tight I felt almost numb, a blaze of heat wicking its way upward and inside, then petering out just as quickly as it started. I'd wanted something, certainly, when I'd asked for this treatment, wanted to go farther than I ever had, shed some layer of skin that's essential for daily life but feels like a cloak during sex, even when I'm naked. I'd wanted something vaguely urgent, something like the Nine Inch Nails line, something like what I'd seen in those porn videos where the girl screams and screams and screams until you don't quite know what's happening to her, only that she cannot live with-out it. But whatever I'd wanted, whatever I'd dreamed about,

Aidan had torched completely. My meek little fantasies were child's play compared to this, were like going to first base when he'd simply upended the whole ballpark. With just his bare hands, his voice, his cock, he *became* an animal for me, one who wouldn't take no for an answer because he didn't even speak any language, let alone English. He became exactly what I hadn't known I needed until then, his paws digging at me, burrowing deep inside, stretching not only my pussy but my boundaries as he bit and dug and pinched and thrust.

My cunt was so perfectly sore, so raw, so hot, that when he finally slammed his cock into me, I went wild. The sounds I let out now were inhuman ones, bubbling up like some deep ancestral wail, coiling forth from my stomach, my cunt, my gut, my memories. My body was pinned beneath him, as much by shock as by force, and I let the tears stream down my cheeks, let him overtake me as his cock seemed to fill my entire body, coursing through me like blood, like power, like magic. Later, I would laugh at how truly out-of-this-world this was, how far removed from our petty punk politics, our little scene, the endless rounds of gossip. Whereas other girls might tattoo their sluttiness across their arms, or their asses, or their chests, the way Aidan fucked me went deeper than any ink ever could. It marked me inside, until I thought I might explode, combusting right there, his prey through and through. He speared me, plunging inside me with all the force he'd been holding in for years, forever possibly, going further than I'd have thought possible, literally and figuratively, smashing me into the floor while my body tried not to escape but to mold to his, to fuse against him so I could feel what he was feeding me forever. As he plundered me, as he fucked me like the animal I'd become, he gave me so much more than his cock, so much more than simply his body. Aidan gave me his darkest self, like a were-wolf or a witch, the kind that only came out at night, under the coveted safety of the dark, a self meant not for public viewing but for me alone. His dark side became mine as we growled at each other, shaking with need until I crumbled first, howling, baying, barking, making noises that were neither animal nor human, but somewhere caught between the two, my body twisted beneath him as I let his power crash over and then through me. I was still quaking when he came, his semen shooting into me like a rocket launching.

And then somehow, after many minutes of silence, of mouths opening and then closing, of words and thoughts gently tiptoeing back into our heads, pushing us over to what humans do best, we smiled at each other. He tumbled onto his back and pulled me on top, and we laughed, while a few errant tears raced down my cheeks. "I think I know what your next tat should be," he said, doodling his finger against my right bicep. "Wild Animal—because you are." Later, he sketched it for me, somehow managing to recreate the essence of what we'd done with elaborate gothic letters, a forest surrounding them, danger signs lurking amid beaded eyes and sharp teeth. For now, I'm just keeping his sketch in my pocket all day, so I can pull it out and look at it and be reminded of him, of us. There are some things I want the world to know about, things I can't stand to have assumed so must emblazon them prominently, but Aidan and I together, well, that's something else entirely. Besides, anyone watching closely enough when I smile just so, making my incisors gleam and my eyes flash, should be able to see the animal in me. And if they don't, they're just not looking closely enough.

ABOUT THE AUTHORS

JANE BLACK lives with her compatibly pervy husband and their three kids in the San Francisco Bay Area. Her erotica and nonfiction have appeared in *Good Vibrations Magazine* (GoodVibes.com). She can be reached at black-janey@yahoo.com.

KATHLEEN BRADEAN's stories can be found in *Amazons: Sexy Tales of Strong Women*, *Best of Best Women's Erotica*, *Blood Surrender*, and *Garden of the Perverse*, as well as *Clean Sheets* and the Erotica Readers and Writer's Association website. Visit her blog at KathleenBradean.blogspot.com.

RACHEL KRAMER BUSSEL is every bit as dirty as her story implies. She serves as Senior Editor at

Penthouse Variations and writes the "Lusty Lady" column for the *Village Voice*. She's editing such anthologies as *Naughty Spanking Stories from A to Z* 1 and 2, *First-Timers*, *Up All Night*, *Ultimate Undies*, *Sexiest Soles*, *Secret Slaves*, *Glamour Girls: Femme/Femme Erotica*, and *Caught Looking: Erotic Tales of Voyeurs and Exhibitionists*. 2007 sees the release of *He's On Top* and *She's On Top*, companion erotica anthologies dedicated to the thrill of dominance, and *Sex and Candy: Sugar Erotica*. Her writing has been published in over sixty anthologies, including *Best American Erotica 2004 and 2006*, as well as *AVN*, *Bust*, Cleansheets.com, *Diva*, *Girlfriends*, *Playgirl*, Mediabistro.com, the *New York Post*, the *San Francisco Chronicle*, *Punk Planet*, and *Zink*. She hosts the monthly In The Flesh Erotic Reading Series in New York City. Visit her at rachelkramerbussel.com.

JEAN CASSE is a Bay Area writer who collects gloves, hand lotions, and antique manicure kits.

JENNIFER CROSS is a writer, writing group facilitator, and member of the erotica collective Dirty Ink. Her stories have appeared in numerous anthologies (in some as Jen Collins), including *Back to Basics*, *Best Fetish Erotica*, *Glamour Girls*, and *Naughty Spanking Stories A-Z* (volume 2). As a survivor of sexual abuse, she is a strong advocate of the beautifully transformative power of smut. She lives and writes in San Francisco.

SCARLETT FRENCH is a short-story writer and a poet. She lives in London's East End with her partner and a pugnacious marmalade cat. She is a dirty bisexual, complete with deviant monogamy. Her erotic fiction has appeared in *Best Lesbian Erotica 2005*, *Va Va Voom*, *First Timers: True Stories of Lesbian Awakening*, and *Travelrotica for Lesbians*. She is currently working on her first novel but is repeatedly distracted by the urge to write filth.

REEN GUIERRE likes sex with a twist. Her steamy stories always end with a little surprise. Her characters—far from being perfect—encounter the unexpected, experience uncertainties, and commit faux pas, but despite the ado, still manage to have great sex. Reen lives with her partner in the north woods where staying toasty warm on a winter's night is as paramount as the pines are tall. Her stories have appeared in *CleanSheets*, *Goodvibes*, and *Oysters and Chocolate* (though not always under the same name). Contact her at reenguierre@yahoo.com.

SUSIE HARA lives and writes in the San Francisco Bay Area. Her stories have appeared in several anthologies, including *Stirring up a Storm*, *Best of Best Women's Erotica*, and *Best American Erotica* (under the pen name Lisa Wolfe). Writing erotic fiction is the most fun she's ever had with a laptop.

THEA HUTCHESON burns up the pages with lust, leather, and latex, brims over with juicy bits in *Best Lesbian Erotica 2001, 2002* and *2006*, *Hot Lesbian Erotica*, *Cthuthlu Sex Magazine*, Amatory-Ink.com, and *Hot Blood XI: Fatal Attractions*. She lives in economically depressed, unscenic, nearly historic Sheridan, Colorado. When she's not hard—or wet—at the computer, she's a Tarot reader and teacher.

KAY JAYBEE is a nomadic thirtysomething with a collection of part-time jobs, who currently happens to be residing in the Grampians of Scotland. She writes during any spare moments she may have, providing she has plenty of black coffee at hand. Her fiction appears in *Lips Like Sugar* as well as *Sex and Music*. She has also recently become a contributor to the erotic website Oysters and Chocolate.

KAYLA KUFFS has been writing BDSM erotica and nonfiction for six years, and is the editor/owner of the online zine *The Dominant's View*. Kayla's writing has appeared in *Whiplash, Leash, Prometheus,* and *Smut* magazines, as well as various websites.

SOPHIE MOUETTE is the pseudonym of two longtime collaborators and long-distance lovers. Her first novel, *Cat Scratch Fever*, was published by Black Lace Books, and she has been published in *Wicked Words* (multiple volumes) and *Best Women's Erotica*, among others. Individually, both authors are multipublished in erotica, SF/F, and romance.

Erotica by TERESA NOELLE ROBERTS has appeared in *Best Women's Erotica 2004* and *2005, Garden of the Perverse*, FishNetmag.com, and many other publications. When not immersed in writing erotica and erotic romance, Teresa is a poet, belly dancer, and medieval reenactor.

RITA ROLLINS is an ex-dancer/model and aspiring erotica writer. She has been published anonymously in *Hustler*; this is her first credited publication. She lives in the Pacific Northwest with her fiancé, who loves to read her bedtime stories.

DONNA GEORGE STOREY has great faith in the magic of words. Her fiction has appeared in *Clean Sheets, Scarlet Letters, Taboo: Forbidden Fantasies for Couples, Foreign Affairs: Erotic Travel Tales, Garden of the Perverse: Fairy Tales for Twisted Adults, The Sexiest Soles: Erotic Stories About Feet and Shoes, Mammoth Book of Best New Erotica* 4 and 5, *Best Women's Erotica* 2005 and 2006, and *Best American Erotica* 2006. Read more of her work at DonnaGeorgeStorey.com.

Called "a trollop with a laptop" by *East Bay Express*, ALISON TYLER is naughty and she knows it. Over the past decade, Ms. Tyler has written more than fifteen explicit novels. Her stories have appeared in anthologies including *Sweet Life I & II, Taboo, Best Women's Erotica* 2002, 2003, and 2005, *Best of Best Women's Erotica, Best Fetish Erotica,* and *Best Lesbian Erotica* 1996, in *Wicked Words 4, 5, 6, 8, and 10,* as well as in *Playgirl Magazine*. Don't miss her latest from Cleis Press, *Exposed: The Erotic Fiction of Alison Tyler*. She is the editor of *Heat Wave, Best Bondage Erotica* (volumes 1 and 2), *Three-Way,* and *Merry Xxxmas* (all from Cleis Press), as well as the *Naughty Stories from A to Z* series (Pretty Things Press). Please visit alisontyler.blogspot.com/.

Born in Cornwall, IRMA WIMPLE currently lives in the Upper Peninsula of Michigan with her seven cats and one tame cougar. A former community college professor, she is a pastry chef by day; at night she is transformed into a torrid and prolific romantic fiction writer. A veteran of five marriages that she considers successful—in that they are over—Irma devotes her time to gardening, ice fishing, reading, and hiking.

JORDANA WINTERS is a Canadian writer whose work has appeared online at eXtasybooks.com, thermoerotic.com, oystersandchocolate.com, and free-sex-story.org. Jordana's writing has also appeared in print form in the anthologies *Best Women's Erotica 2006, Uniform Sex,* and *Erotic Tales.* When not hiding behind her computer telling filthy tales, Jordana is an often disgruntled white-collar worker. She spends much of her time reading, writing, doing as much and as little as possible, and pissing people off. Her website is jordanawinters.tripod.com.

KRISTINA WRIGHT's short fiction has been published in over thirty anthologies, including *Best Women's Erotica 2000,* four editions of the Lambda-award-winning series *Best Lesbian Erotica, Sweet Life: Erotic Fantasies for Couples, Amazons: Sexy Tales of Strong Women,* the *Mammoth Book of Best New Erotica* (volume 5), *Blood Sisters: Lesbian Vampire Tales, Ultimate Undies: Erotic Stories About Lingerie and Underwear,* and *Secret Slaves: Erotic Stories of Bondage.* Her writing has also been featured in the nonfiction guide the *Many Joys of Sex Toys* and in e-zines such as *Clean Sheets, Scarlet Letters,* and *Good Vibes Magazine.* Kristina lives in Virginia with her husband and a menagerie of pets and is currently pursuing a graduate degree in humanities. For more information about Kristina's life and writing, visit her website, kristinawright.com. And no, she has never made an obscene phone call, no matter what anyone says to the contrary.

ABOUT THE EDITOR

VIOLET BLUE is a professional sex educator, sex columnist, female porn expert, and pro-porn pundit. She is an author at Metblogs SF and is "girl Friday" contributor at Fleshbot.com. She is the editor of the Cleis Press anthologies *Best Women's Erotica* series, along with *Best Sex Writing 2005, Sweet Life: Erotic Fantasies for Couples, Sweet Life 2, Taboo: Forbidden Fantasies for Couples*, and *Lips Like Sugar: Women's Erotic Fantasies.* She is the author of many sex guides from Cleis Press, including the *Smart Girl's Guide to Porn*, the *Adventurous Couple's Guide to Sex Toys*, the *Ultimate Guide to Adult Videos*, the *Ultimate Guide to Sexual Fantasy*, the *Ultimate Guide to Fellatio*, and the *Ultimate Guide to Cunnilingus*, the latter two of which have been translated into

French, Spanish, and Russian. Blue has appeared on Playboy TV's *Sexcetera,* NPR, and CNN, and she has been featured in such publications as *Esquire, Cosmopolitan, O, The Oprah Magazine,* Salon.com, *Newsweek,* the *Wall Street Journal,* and *Wired.* Visit her website at tinynibbles.com, or listen to her podcast, Open Source Sex.

Best Women's Erotica

Ordering is easy! Call us toll free to place your MC/VISA order or mail the order form below with payment to: Cleis Press, P.O. Box 14697, San Francisco, CA 94114.

ORDER FORM

Buy 4 books, Get 1 FREE*

QTY	TITLE	PRICE
_____	_____	_____
_____	_____	_____
_____	_____	_____
_____	_____	_____
_____	_____	_____
_____	_____	_____
_____	_____	_____
_____	_____	_____
_____	_____	_____
_____	_____	_____
_____	_____	_____

SUBTOTAL _____

SHIPPING _____

SALES TAX _____

TOTAL _____

Add $3.95 postage/handling for the first book ordered and $1.00 for each additional book. Outside North America, please contact us for shipping rates. California residents add 8.5% sales tax. Payment in U.S. dollars only.

* Free book of equal or lesser value. Shipping and applicable sales tax extra.
Cleis Press • (800) 780-2279 • orders@cleispress.com
www.cleispress.com
You'll find more great books on our website